JUNIOR JINX
A PARANORMAL HOLIDAY ROMANCE

NORTH POLE UNIVERSITY
BOOK FOUR

MARIE-HELENE LEBEAULT

BEACHES AND TRAILS
PUBLISHING

CONTENTS

CHAPTER ONE

THE BINDING CURSE

IVY

The potion exploded.

Not metaphorically, not dramatically, literally exploded, sending shards of crystal cauldron flying across Professor Frostwick's Advanced Magical Applications lab and coating half the workspace in what had been perfectly measured winter mint essence three seconds ago.

Outside the laboratory's tall windows, fresh snow was beginning to fall, the kind of soft, persistent flakes that marked the start of NPU's winter term. The scent of peppermint candles from the corridor mixed with the sharp, acrid smell of magical mishap, creating an oddly festive backdrop for complete chaos.

I ducked behind my lab station as chaos erupted around me. Other students scrambled away from the blast radius, their protective charms flaring to life in brilliant displays of defensive magic. Being the smallest sprite in the lab usually meant slipping under the radar during these disasters. Not today. The acrid smell of burnt herbs and ozone filled the air, mixing with the sharp scent of magical mishap that made my sprite instincts prick with alarm.

"Everyone remain calm!" Professor Frostwick's voice cut through the pandemonium, her ice magic already working to contain the worst of the damage. Frost spread across the spilled potion, neutralizing its effects before it could eat through the laboratory floor. "Protective barriers up until we can assess..."

But I wasn't listening anymore. Because there, glinting among the crystal shards scattered across my workspace, was something that definitely hadn't been in my cauldron thirty seconds ago.

A charm. Small, intricate, and pulsing with the kind of dark energy that made my light magic recoil instinctively. It looked like a miniature snowflake carved from black ice, its delicate edges seeming to absorb the laboratory's bright illumination. Even from here, I could feel how massive its magical presence was, like a thundercloud compressed into something barely larger than my thumb.

Without thinking, because if I'd thought about it, I would have known better, I reached for it.

The moment my fingers closed around the charm, pain lanced up my arm like frozen lightning. The world tilted sideways, colors bleeding together as magical energy I didn't recognize flooded my system. I heard someone scream, distantly realized it might have been me, and then,

Connection.

His power crashed into me like an avalanche. I was a snowflake caught in its path, fragile, tiny, completely overwhelmed by the sheer magnitude of magic that dwarfed everything I'd ever imagined. Not the gentle, willing partnership magic I'd read about in theoretical texts. This was raw, violent, involuntary, a magical tether that snapped into place between my consciousness and someone else's with all the subtlety of a colliding sleigh.

The charm fused to my wrist with a flash of silver light that left afterimages dancing across my vision. Where it touched my skin, intricate runes began to appear, spiraling up my forearm in patterns that looked ancient and definitely not sanctioned by any curriculum I'd studied.

"What..." I started to say, then stopped as the connection stabilized and I felt it. Him. Another magical presence linked to mine through bonds I hadn't chosen and couldn't break.

And he was not happy about it.

Fury crashed into my consciousness, controlled, arctic, and so intense it should have flattened me completely. But somehow, impossibly, his anger felt... steadying. Like the eye of a hurricane where I could finally catch my breath. Followed immediately by something that might have been fear, though it was wrapped in so many layers of protective ice I couldn't be certain.

Of all the sprites, a voice said in my head, not my voice, definitely masculine, and radiating the kind of bitter resignation usually reserved for students who'd just realized they'd failed their final exams. *Why did it have to be him?*

Wait. That wasn't right. I was the one thinking about sprites. The voice in my head was thinking about sprites. Which meant,

"Miss Snowfall!" Professor Frostwick's sharp tone cut through my magical vertigo. "Step away from whatever you're holding this instant!"

But I couldn't step away. Couldn't even move. Because the binding rune was still flaring with power, and through it, I could feel another magical signature responding to mine. Dark frost meeting ice-bright light in a chaotic dance that made both our powers spike unpredictably.

Books began flying.

Not in any organized pattern, just sudden, violent motion as the unstable magic radiating from the charm affected every enchanted object in the laboratory. Cauldrons rattled on their stands like sleigh bells caught in a windstorm. The carefully cultivated ice gardens along the windows cracked and reformed into strange, twisted shapes. Professor Frostwick's demonstration materials developed a life of their own, zooming around the room like caffeinated pixies. Even the decorative holly wreaths that lined the laboratory's upper walls began to shake loose, their enchanted berries scattering across the floor in tiny explosions of red light.

"Everyone out!" Professor Frostwick commanded, her own magic blazing as she tried to contain the chaos. "Now!"

Students fled toward the exits, but I remained frozen at my lab station, transfixed by the feeling of someone else's magic intertwining with mine whether I wanted it to or not. The runes on my arm pulsed in rhythm with a heartbeat that wasn't my own, and through the unwanted connection, I caught flashes of sensation that didn't belong to me.

Stone corridors. The scent of winter storms. A deep, bone-crushing loneliness that made my chest ache with sympathy I couldn't afford to feel.

Then footsteps, quick and purposeful, approaching the laboratory from the main corridor.

The door burst open, and Rowan Blackthorn stalked into the chaos.

I'd seen him around campus, of course. Everyone had. He was impossible to miss, tall, dark-haired, and wrapped in the kind of winter magic that made other students unconsciously step aside when he passed. There were stories about his family, whispers about curses and political complications that followed the Blackthorn name like persistent shadows.

But I'd never seen him up close. Had never noticed the sharp intelligence in his pale eyes, shouldn't have been noticing it now, with everything in chaos, or the way he moved like a storm barely contained in human form. All that power compressed into a frame that still managed to make me feel like a sparrow facing a winter tempest. I should have been looking away, focusing on the crisis, but something about his presence made it impossible to think about anything else. Had definitely never felt his magic responding to mine with recognition that bypassed conscious thought entirely.

He stopped three feet away from my lab station, his gaze fixed on the charm fused to my wrist, and said the last words I expected to hear from the campus's most notorious loner:

"We have a problem."

The casual certainty in his voice made something inside me want to either laugh hysterically or throw something at his head. Here I was, bound by magic I didn't understand to someone I'd never spoken to, and he sounded like he was discussing a mildly inconvenient scheduling conflict. How could he be so calm when my entire world had just tilted off its axis?

The binding rune flared again, brighter this time, and I felt our magical signatures lock into alignment. Not harmony, that would come later, if it came at all. This was recognition, acknowledgment, the first note of a song neither of us had chosen to sing.

Around us, the laboratory's chaos intensified. Crystal equipment vibrated with sympathetic resonance. The remaining potions in their storage alcoves began to glow with borrowed power. Even Professor Frostwick's containment spells wavered as whatever force had created the binding between us fed on the magical energy in the room.

"Can you break it?" I asked, lifting my arm to show him the runes that now decorated my skin like intricate silver tattoos.

Rowan's expression went darker than winter midnight. "If I could break it, do you think I'd be standing here?"

Through the bond, I felt the truth he wasn't saying: he'd already tried. Had felt the binding snap into place from wherever he'd been on campus and had attempted every severing spell he knew before making his way to the laboratory.

Nothing had worked. If anything, his efforts had only made the connection stronger.

Which should have terrified me. Instead, hearing his thoughts in my head felt oddly... right. Like finding the missing piece of a song I hadn't realized was incomplete.

"Then what do we..."

The laboratory door flew open again, this time revealing Dylan Vixen and Lyra Lumina. They took in the scene with quick, professional assessment, the magical chaos, the binding rune on my wrist, the way Rowan and I stood frozen in place by forces neither of us understood.

"Right," Dylan said with the kind of cheerful resignation that suggested this wasn't his first encounter with uncontrolled magical phenomena. "Looks like we're dealing with an ancient binding situation. Lyra, thoughts?"

Lyra was already moving, her light magic blazing as she began analyzing the energy patterns radiating from the charm. "Definitely pre-institutional. The magical signature suggests Winter Court origins, probably designed as a political bonding tool rather than a romantic one."

"Political bonding?" I squeaked.

"Think arranged marriage," Dylan said helpfully, "but with magic doing the arranging."

My stomach dropped. "And the compulsion part?"

"Right, that." Dylan's fox-shifter grin turned slightly apologetic. "If you try to fight it too hard, both participants risk magical backlash that could permanently damage your casting abilities."

The rune on my wrist pulsed, as if responding to the explanation, and I felt another wave of Rowan's controlled fury crash into my consciousness.

This is exactly what my family would do, his mental voice was tight with bitter familiarity, but it resonated through me like a perfectly tuned bell. *Ancient magic, no choice, no escape clause.*

A chill ran down my spine that had nothing to do with the laboratory's temperature. There was something beneath his words, a darkness, a weight that spoke of secrets far more dangerous than simple family politics. Whatever the Blackthorns were involved in, it was deeper and more frightening than campus rumors suggested.

Your family did this? I thought back at him, not entirely certain the bond worked both ways.

His pale eyes flicked to mine, and I felt his surprise that I'd heard him clearly. *Someone in my family's political circle. The question is whether they were targeting you or me.*

"Both," Lyra said grimly, having caught enough of our mental exchange to follow the conversation. "Ancient political bindings were designed to create alliances between magical houses. If someone wanted to neutralize two potentially powerful students..."

She didn't finish the thought, but she didn't need to. The implication hung in the air like a winter storm waiting to break.

Someone had wanted to tie us together, whether we were compatible or not. Someone had decided our magical futures without consulting us. Someone had turned what should have been a choice into a trap.

The charm pulsed again, and this time the magical backlash was strong enough to crack the laboratory's reinforced windows.

Professor Frostwick, who had been maintaining her containment spells with impressive determination, finally looked at Dylan and Lyra with something approaching desperation.

"Can you stabilize this before they bring down half the academic wing?"

"We can try," Lyra said. "But they're going to need somewhere private to work through the initial binding adjustment. The Observatory?"

Dylan nodded. "Observatory. Away from other students, plenty of space for magical mishaps, and all your partnership research equipment."

I looked at Rowan, who was watching the conversation with the expression of someone who'd just realized his life had taken a sharp turn into territory he'd never wanted to explore.

Through the bond, I caught the edge of his thoughts: *Partnership magic. Of course. Because being magically bound to a sprite I've never spoken to wasn't complicated enough.*

I can hear you, you know, I thought back at him, letting some of my own irritation bleed through the connection.

His eyebrows rose slightly. *Good. Then you heard the part about this not being my choice either.*

Loud and clear.

Despite everything, the chaos, the unwanted binding, the fact that my junior year had just taken a dramatic turn toward the impossible, I felt my mouth twitch with something that might have been amusement.

If we were stuck with each other, we might as well start with honesty.

The charm pulsed one more time, and I swore I felt it... settle. Not disappear, not weaken, but accept the current situation as the new normal.

Magic, apparently, had its own opinion about what constituted proper introductions.

CHAPTER TWO
STORM IN HUMAN FORM

ROWAN

The binding hit me like a lightning strike while I was practicing defensive magic in the abandoned tower where nobody could witness what my family's legacy had made me.

One moment, I was containing another bout of the nightmare frost that had been getting worse each week, ice magic twisted into something hungry and cruel, the way it always turned when the Blackthorn curse decided to remind me of my place in the world. The next, foreign magic crashed into my consciousness with all the subtlety of an avalanche.

Light magic. Bright, chaotic, and utterly unprepared for what it had just connected itself to.

I'd dropped my practice wands and was running before I'd even processed what had happened. The binding rune burned against my ribs, where it had materialized through my shirt like a brand, pulling me toward whoever had been unfortunate enough to trigger whatever ancient trap my family had set this time.

The sensation was unlike anything I'd experienced before, not just a magical connection, but emotional resonance. Through the unwanted bond, I could feel her panic, her confusion, the way her magic was spiraling out of control as it tried to process what had just happened to her. What had just happened to us.

It should have been invasive, overwhelming. Instead, it felt oddly... stabilizing. Like my storm magic had found an anchor it didn't know it needed.

The Winter Court had been playing these games for centuries, and the Blackthorns were their most reliable instruments. The only question was whether they'd been targeting me or some other poor soul, and which had been the true objective.

The laboratory door was already smoking when I arrived, Professor Frostwick's containment spells working overtime to keep whatever magical chaos was happening inside from spreading to the rest of the academic wing. Holly berries from the corridor's festive decorations crunched under my boots, apparently, the magical backlash had been strong enough to shake loose even the enchanted wreaths three rooms away. Through the frosted glass, I could see shapes moving frantically, books flying in erratic patterns, the telltale shimmer of unstable magic running wild.

And through the unwanted connection now linking my consciousness to someone else's, I felt her.

Terror. Confusion. The desperate need to understand what was happening, layered over a determination that should have been impossible for someone whose magical signature felt no larger than a candle flame.

But there was something else, too. Something that made my storm magic respond with interest rather than its usual defensive hostility. Her light wasn't trying to banish my darkness or fix what was broken in my magical core. It was simply... there. Present. Steady despite her fear.

A sprite. Of all the students at North Pole University, the binding had attached itself to a sprite barely strong enough to register on most magical detection spells.

Perfect. Absolutely perfect. As if my family's political machinations weren't complicated enough without involving someone who'd probably never even heard of the Winter Court feuds that had shaped the last three centuries of Blackthorn history.

But as I pushed through the laboratory door, my storm magic automatically spreading out to assess the situation, I had to revise that initial assessment. The chaos was worse than I'd expected, not just books flying, but cauldrons rattling like trapped spirits, ice gardens fracturing into dangerous shards, even the decorative holly wreaths shaking apart in showers of enchanted berries. And at the center of it all stood the smallest student I'd ever seen, barely visible behind an overturned lab station but refusing to back down.

Not cowering. Not fleeing like the other students had. Standing there with her chin lifted and her frost-colored eyes blazing with the kind of defiance that suggested she might be small in stature, but she was not small in spirit.

She couldn't have been more than five feet tall, with silver-white hair that caught the laboratory's chaotic light patterns and skin that seemed to glow with its own inner radiance. Then Professor Frostwick's voice cut through the chaos: "Miss Snowfall! Step away from whatever you're holding this instant!"

Ivy Snowfall. Even through the magical mayhem surrounding us, she looked luminous. Delicate as spun glass, but with something in her pale blue eyes that suggested she was far tougher than her appearance implied.

The binding rune on her wrist was definitely Blackthorn work, I recognized the cruel elegance of the design, the way it pulsed with energy meant to control rather than connect. Someone in my family's sphere had decided this tiny sprite would serve their purposes, whether she wanted to or not.

The fury that rose in response was cold, controlled, and absolutely murderous. Not just because someone had trapped her in this situation without her consent, but because they'd used her to trap me as well. Ancient magic, designed to force bonds that should have been chosen freely.

"We have a problem," I said, because there was no point in pretending this was anything other than exactly what it looked like. Though I had to admit, being magically bound to someone I'd never spoken to was a new low, even by Blackthorn standards.

She stared at me with those frost-colored eyes, and I caught the edge of her thoughts through our unwanted connection. I shouldn't have been noticing the way her gaze held steady against mine even while the room collapsed around us, but I was. Irritation at my calm tone, confusion about why I wasn't falling apart the way she was, and underneath it all, something that might have been recognition.

How can he be so calm when my entire world has just tilted off its axis?

Because I'd been expecting this my entire life. Because Blackthorns don't get the luxury of falling apart when the family's political games finally catch up with them. Because someone had to stay functional long enough to figure out how we were both going to survive whatever trap had just snapped shut around us.

But looking at her, really looking at her for the first time, I felt something crack in my carefully maintained composure. She was so small, so unprepared for the darkness that came with my family name.

"Can you break it?" she asked, lifting her arm to show me the runes that now decorated her skin like intricate silver tattoos.

If I could break it, I would have done so the moment the

binding snapped into place. I'd tried every severing spell in my considerable repertoire during my sprint across campus, then several that were definitely not approved for student use. Advanced magic that would have made Professor Blitzen expel me on the spot if she'd witnessed it.

Nothing had worked. If anything, my efforts had strengthened the connection between us, as if the binding was designed to feed on attempts to break it.

Which, knowing my family's approach to magical contracts, it probably was.

"If I could break it, do you think I'd be standing here?" I replied, letting some of my own frustration bleed into my voice.

Through the bond, I felt her reaction to my honesty, surprise that I wasn't trying to reassure her, followed by something that might have been relief that at least one of us was being straightforward about our situation.

Then Dylan Vixen and Lyra Lumina appeared in the laboratory doorway, and I had to resist the urge to laugh at the absurdity of it all. Of course, the campus's most famous partnership magic researchers would show up to analyze my family's latest disaster.

"Right," Dylan said with that cheerful fox-shifter energy that suggested he found magical chaos personally entertaining. "Looks like we're dealing with an ancient binding situation. Lyra, thoughts?"

Lyra was already moving, her light magic blazing as she examined the energy patterns radiating from the charm fused to the sprite's wrist. Her analysis was quick, professional, and unfortunately accurate.

"Definitely pre-institutional. The magical signature suggests Winter Court origins, probably designed as a political bonding tool rather than a romantic one."

The sprite, Ivy, squeaked out a question about political bonding, and Dylan's explanation was characteristically blunt.

"Think arranged marriage, but with magic doing the arranging."

I watched her face go pale as the implications sank in, felt her stomach drop through our unwanted connection. She was realizing, as I already had, that this wasn't some random magical accident. Someone had targeted us specifically.

The question was why. What did anyone gain by binding together a Blackthorn heir with a sprite who'd probably spent her entire academic career trying to stay invisible? Unless...

Unless someone wanted to neutralize us both, remove two potentially problematic students from the political equation by trapping them in a bond that would either destroy them or render them too distracted to interfere with larger plans.

"And the compulsion part?" she asked.

Dylan's apologetic grin didn't soften the blow. "Right, that. If you try to fight it too hard, both participants risk magical backlash that could permanently damage your casting abilities."

The binding rune pulsed, as if responding to the explanation, and I felt another wave of her distress crash into my consciousness. But underneath the fear and confusion, there was something else. Something that reminded me why the Blackthorn family motto was *"Winter endures"* rather than *"Winter surrenders."* She was scared, but she wasn't going to break. Whatever else Ivy Snowfall was, she had steel in her spine.

And through our bond, I could feel her beginning to realize the same thing about me. That, despite my family's reputation, despite the shadows that followed the Blackthorn name, I wasn't the monster she'd probably been expecting.

This is exactly what my family would do, I thought, not bothering to shield the mental communication from her. *Ancient magic, no choice, no escape clause.*

Your family did this? Her mental voice was sharp with accusation.

Someone in my family's political circle. The question is whether they were targeting you or me.

I felt her shiver as the words settled between us, sensed her picking up on the shadows I wasn't ready to explain. The Blackthorn curse wasn't common knowledge, but it cast darkness that sensitive people could feel even when they didn't understand what they were sensing.

And Ivy, despite her size, was clearly more sensitive to magical undercurrents than most. She might not know the details of my family's legacy, but she understood that whatever bound us together was more dangerous than simple political maneuvering.

Lyra's analysis confirmed what I'd already suspected, this was targeting both of us, designed to create an alliance whether we wanted one or not. The kind of maneuvering that had kept the Winter Court in power for centuries.

The charm pulsed again, and this time the magical backlash was strong enough to crack the laboratory's reinforced windows. Professor Frostwick's containment spells wavered dangerously.

"Can you stabilize this before they bring down half the academic wing?" she asked Dylan and Lyra, her voice barely controlled with desperation.

"We can try," Lyra said. "But they're going to need somewhere private to work through the initial binding adjustment. The Observatory?"

The Observatory. Where Dylan and Lyra had apparently spent the last semester proving that partnership magic could work when both participants chose it freely, the irony wasn't lost on me.

But as we prepared to leave the destroyed laboratory, something had shifted in the magical chaos around us. The books had stopped flying. The cauldrons had quieted. Even the fractured ice gardens seemed to be stabilizing.

Not because the binding had weakened, if anything, the connection between Ivy and me felt stronger than ever. But it was no longer fighting itself. Our magical signatures were beginning to synchronize despite our resistance, finding harmony where there should have been discord.

It felt too natural. Too easy. Like we'd been designed to complement each other, which should have been impossible given that we'd never even spoken before today.

That kind of magical compatibility didn't happen by accident.

As we prepared to leave the destroyed laboratory, I caught Ivy watching me with an expression I couldn't quite read. Wariness, certainly. Curiosity, despite herself. And something else, a flicker of awareness that this connection between us felt more natural than it should have, given that it had been forced on us by magic and manipulation.

Partnership magic for unwilling partners, Lyra had said to Dylan, and I'd felt Ivy's reaction through our bond. Not just fear, but a tiny spark of something that might have been hope.

Dangerous thinking for both of us.

I was a Blackthorn, cursed bloodline and Winter Court politics wrapped in storm magic. She was someone who'd clearly spent her life avoiding attention rather than courting the kind of power that came with danger.

We were the worst possible match, bound by magic that cared nothing for our preferences.

But as we followed Dylan and Lyra toward the Observatory, I couldn't shake the feeling that whoever had orchestrated this binding had made one crucial miscalculation.

They'd assumed we'd fight it. Fight each other. Let the forced connection tear us both apart rather than find a way to make it work.

They'd never considered the possibility that winter storms and bright light might actually complement each other, if given the chance.

The binding rune burned against my ribs, settling into a rhythm that matched Ivy's heartbeat, and for the first time since the connection had snapped into place, I allowed myself to wonder:

What if this wasn't a trap?

What if it was an opportunity?

Maybe light wasn't meant to banish storms. Maybe it was meant to illuminate them.

CHAPTER THREE
CAMPUS CHAOS

IVY

The Observatory should have felt like a sanctuary.

Lyra had welcomed us into her research space with the kind of professional warmth that suggested she genuinely wanted to help rather than simply studying us like fascinating specimens. Dylan had conjured comfortable seating and hot chocolate that tasted like liquid comfort, complete with marshmallows that reformed themselves every time they melted. The space itself hummed with peaceful energy, its crystalline surfaces and soft aurora patterns intended to be soothing.

Instead, I felt like I was sitting on a powder keg.

Not because of the magical chaos, surprisingly, that had settled the moment Rowan and I had taken seats across from each other at Lyra's main research table. The binding rune on my wrist had stopped its frantic pulsing, settling into a steady rhythm that matched my heartbeat. Even the strange echo of Rowan's thoughts in my head had quieted to a manageable whisper.

No, the problem was that everything felt too normal. Too

comfortable. Like my magic had decided this was exactly where it wanted to be, regardless of the circumstances that had brought us here.

"The good news," Lyra said, her light magic dancing around her fingers as she analyzed the binding rune's energy signature, "is that this isn't a destructive binding. It's designed for enhancement rather than control."

"Enhancement?" I squeaked.

"Think of it like magical amplification," Dylan explained, perching on the edge of Lyra's desk with the casual confidence of someone who'd clearly spent many hours in this space. "Your individual casting abilities should become stronger when you're working together, not weaker."

"And the bad news?" Rowan asked, his voice carrying that sardonic edge I was already learning to recognize.

Lyra's expression grew troubled. "The binding is ancient enough that we don't have complete documentation of its effects. It's also tied to emotional resonance, as well as magical compatibility. The stronger your connection becomes, the more... integrated your magical signatures will be."

Through our bond, I felt Rowan's sharp spike of concern. *Integrated how?*

That's what we need to find out, I thought back, then caught myself. Was I already getting used to the mental connection? That seemed like something I should be more worried about.

"We'll start with basic compatibility tests," Lyra continued. "Simple spellwork, both individual and collaborative. We need to understand how the binding affects your magic before we can determine whether it's safe to maintain or if we need to find a way to modify it."

"Modify it?" I asked hopefully.

"Breaking it isn't an option," Dylan said gently. "Not without risking serious magical backlash for both of you. But we might be able to adjust the parameters, make it less intrusive."

Less intrusive would be good. The constant awareness of Rowan's emotional state was already proving distracting. Right now, for instance, I could feel his carefully controlled anxiety beneath his calm exterior, along with something that might have been protectiveness whenever Dylan or Lyra directed questions at me.

Which was... unexpected. And confusing. And definitely something I shouldn't be finding as comforting as I was.

"Let's start simple," Lyra suggested. "Ivy, can you create a basic light construct? Something you'd be comfortable with in any normal class situation."

I nodded, extending my hand and calling up the kind of illumination spell I'd been practicing since my first year at NPU. Light magic was supposed to be instinctive for sprites, we were creatures of luminescence, after all. But I'd always struggled with the advanced techniques that came naturally to my classmates. My light constructs tended to be small, dim, and disappointingly brief.

This time was different.

The moment I reached for my magic, I felt Rowan's power respond through our bond. Not interfering, not overwhelming, just... supporting. Like someone had suddenly provided a stable foundation for abilities that had always felt precarious.

The light that bloomed from my palm was three times brighter than anything I'd ever produced, and it held its form with perfect stability. Instead of my usual flickering candle flame, I'd created what looked like a miniature star.

"Whoa," Dylan breathed.

"How does that feel?" Lyra asked, her academic excitement barely contained.

"Strong," I admitted, staring at the radiant construct hovering above my hand. "Really strong. Like my magic finally has room to grow."

Through our connection, I felt Rowan's surprise matching my own. Whatever he'd been expecting from our forced partnership, this level of enhancement hadn't been it.

"Rowan, your turn," Lyra said. "Can you show us a basic frost spell?"

I watched him extend his hand, noting the careful control in every movement. When his magic manifested, I understood why.

His frost wasn't like the pretty, decorative ice magic I'd seen from other winter students. This was something darker, hungrier, patterns that seemed to absorb light rather than reflect it, creating shadows within shadows that made my sprite instincts prick with unease.

But the moment our magical signatures touched through the binding, everything changed. My light magic didn't banish his shadows, it illuminated them, revealing the intricate beauty hidden within the darkness. His frost became crystalline art, complex and mesmerizing rather than threatening.

"Extraordinary," Lyra murmured, her research instincts clearly in overdrive. "Your magical signatures are creating compound enhancement. Ivy, your light provides structural support for Rowan's more complex ice work. Rowan, your magic gives Ivy's illumination depth and staying power."

"So we're actually... compatible?" I asked hesitantly.

"More than compatible. You're complementary." Dylan's fox-shifter grin was bright with genuine pleasure. "This is the kind of magical partnership that theory texts dream about but rarely document in practice."

I should have felt relieved. Happy, even. Instead, a knot of anxiety was forming in my stomach. I'd spent three years trying not to be noticed, content to be the smallest sprite in any room rather than risk the kind of attention that came with standing out. And now everyone was staring at me like I'd just lit the aurora myself.

"Can we try something more advanced?" Lyra asked, her academic excitement barely contained. "Perhaps a collaborative defensive ward?"

"Maybe we should pace ourselves," I said hesitantly, though I was curious about what else we might be able to accomplish together.

"Just one more test," Lyra coaxed. "Defensive magic is crucial for partnership assessments."

Dylan leaned forward with interest. "Protective wards are notoriously difficult to coordinate between different magical types. If you two can manage it..."

"We'll try," Rowan said, though I could feel his wariness through our bond.

Lyra gestured for us to stand facing each other. "The technique requires synchronized intent and magical timing. Most students need weeks of practice to achieve basic coordination."

I extended my hands toward Rowan, and he mirrored the gesture. When our palms almost touched, I felt that familiar surge of connection, stronger now that we were focusing deliberately on magical collaboration.

"Create a barrier together," Lyra instructed. "Ivy, project light outward. Rowan, weave frost to reinforce and contain."

I called up my magic, letting light pour from my palms in steady streams. But instead of forming the weak, flickering barrier I'd expected, the illumination blazed with confidence I'd never possessed. Through our bond, I felt Rowan responding, his frost magic spiraling around my light like intricate silver filigree.

The ward that materialized between us was breathtaking, a

shimmering wall of luminous ice that looked like captured starlight, both beautiful and clearly impenetrable.

"Well," Dylan said after a moment of stunned silence. "That's the most aesthetically pleasing defensive barrier I've ever witnessed."

"And probably the strongest," Lyra added, moving closer to examine the ward's construction. "The magical density readings are off the charts."

"It feels effortless," I admitted, staring at our creation in wonder. "Like my magic knows exactly what to do when his is there to support it."

"Same," Rowan said, and through our connection, I felt his amazement matching mine. "Usually, my frost magic fights any attempt at collaboration. It's designed to work independently, pushing other elements aside. But with yours..."

"It becomes something new," I finished.

"Something better," Dylan observed with a grin. "Though if you two keep making breakthrough discoveries, Lyra's going to want to study you for the rest of the semester."

"Of course," Lyra said immediately. "This is a lot to absorb. Rowan, why don't you stay here and help me verify these readings? Dylan can take Ivy up to the observation deck for some fresh air."

I felt Rowan's immediate tension through our bond, we'd just discovered we couldn't be apart for more than fifteen minutes, but Lyra was already pulling up monitoring displays that would clearly benefit from his frost magic expertise.

"It's just three floors up," Dylan said, catching my hesitation. "Fifteen minutes, tops. We'll test whether vertical distance matters differently than horizontal."

Dylan bounced to his feet with characteristic energy, though I noticed he was checking a chronometer. "Come on, Ivy. The

Observatory has the best view of the campus aurora patterns, especially during the winter term. And we'll time this carefully."

As we followed him toward a crystalline staircase that spiraled up into the Observatory's upper levels, I caught Rowan's eye. Through our connection, I sensed his gratitude that I hadn't pushed for more testing, along with a hint of approval for my ability to read the situation.

Thank you, his mental voice was quieter than usual. *I needed a moment to think.*

Me too, I admitted. *This is all happening very fast.*

The observation deck was breathtaking, a circular platform enclosed in transparent crystal that provided a panoramic view of North Pole University's snow-covered campus. In the distance, the aurora borealis danced across the sky in ribbons of green and gold, while closer to the ground, magical lights from various buildings created their own constellation of warm illumination.

"Beautiful, isn't it?" Dylan said, settling onto one of the cushioned benches that lined the deck's perimeter. "Lyra comes up here when she needs to think. Says the bigger perspective helps with problem-solving."

I could understand that. From up here, the campus looked peaceful, organized, magical in all the best ways. It was easy to forget about binding runes and forced partnerships and the way my magic had just performed feats I'd never thought possible.

Through the Observatory's communication crystal, Rowan's voice came through from the upper monitoring station where he'd gone with Lyra.

"Dylan, what happens if word about this gets out? About our... compatibility?"

Even separated by three floors, I could feel his worry through our bond, though the distance was starting to make my binding rune ache with warning.

Dylan's expression grew more serious as he glanced between the communication crystal and me. "You're worried about attention from the wrong people."

"The Blackthorn name attracts certain kinds of interest," I say, Rowan's earlier words coming back to mind.

"Political interest. The kind that tends to complicate students' academic experiences."

Through our bond, I felt the weight of whatever he wasn't saying, amplified by the growing discomfort of separation. Family complications. Court politics. Secrets that ran deeper than simple magical abilities.

"And Ivy's safety becomes a concern if people think she's connected to those complications," Dylan finished, understanding immediately. He touched the crystal. "Rowan, you should come back down. Your rune's starting to flare, isn't it?"

My stomach dropped. I hadn't even considered that angle. Being bound to Rowan didn't just mean enhanced magic and mental connection, it meant inheriting whatever enemies his family had made over the centuries.

"We'll be careful about who we involve," Dylan promised. "Lyra's research stays confidential unless you both consent to publication. And we'll work on finding ways to help you manage the binding without drawing attention."

"What about classes?" I asked, suddenly realizing another complication had arisen. "If our magic is enhanced when we're together, what happens when we're apart? Will I go back to barely being able to light a candle?"

"That's... a really good question," Dylan admitted. "And something we'll need to test carefully."

As if summoned by my anxiety, the binding rune on my wrist began to pulse with warning. Not painful, exactly, but insistent. Like it was trying to tell me something urgent.

"What is it?" Rowan asked, immediately moving closer.

"I'm not sure. The rune just started..." I gasped as the sensation intensified, spreading up my entire arm. Not just my magic reaching for something it couldn't find. My whole being was straining toward Rowan, like every part of me recognized he was too far away.

The Observatory's alarm system activated with a sound like crystalline bells shattering. Emergency lights began flashing, and through the observation deck's transparent walls, we could see students running across the campus grounds.

"That's the magical emergency signal," Dylan said, his casual demeanor instantly shifting to alert tension. "Something's gone wrong in one of the academic buildings."

Through our bond, I felt Rowan's grim realization matching my growing horror. "It's connected to us, isn't it? The binding?"

As if in answer, my rune flared bright enough to be visible through my sleeve, and the desperate reaching sensation intensified.

"How long have we been apart?" Rowan asked, though I could see he was already calculating.

"Fifteen minutes," I said. "Since you went with Lyra to check the upper-level monitors while I stayed here with Dylan."

"That might be the threshold," Dylan realized, his voice tight with concern.

"The binding isn't just enhanced when you're together...it's unstable when you're separated beyond a certain distance or time limit."

Through the observation deck's crystal walls, we could see magical chaos spreading across the campus. Lights flickering in dormitory windows. Students abandoning their evening activities to deal with some kind of emergency. Even from this distance, the aurora patterns above the campus looked agitated, swirling in configurations that definitely weren't natural.

"We need to get back to Lyra," Dylan said urgently. "Now."

But as we rushed toward the Observatory's main level, the horrible realization settling in my chest felt heavier than ice. This binding wasn't just about enhancement and compatibility. It was about dependence.

We weren't just magically stronger together. We were magically unstable apart.

Which meant that whatever freedom I'd thought I still had, whatever choices I'd imagined I could make about my own life and academic future, they'd just disappeared along with any hope of returning to my comfortable invisibility.

The binding rune pulsed again, more urgently this time, and through the Observatory's crystal walls, I could hear the distant sound of emergency bells echoing across our campus.

The campus where some kinds of magic apparently didn't care what you wanted or needed or feared.

Where some kinds of magic just took what they wanted, whether you were ready or not.

CHAPTER FOUR

STORM AND SANCTUARY

ROWAN

The moment we reached the Observatory's main level, I knew
we were too late to prevent the crisis, but hopefully not too late to
contain it.

Lyra was standing at her central console, her light magic
blazing as she tracked magical disturbances across multiple
displays. The readings showed chaos spreading from the academic wing outward, power fluctuations in the dormitories,
unstable aurora patterns above the campus, portal fireplaces
hiccuping in the transportation network. A couple misfired to the
Village and right back, classic loop glitch. Even the enchanted
sleigh systems showed signs of disruption.

"How bad is it?" Dylan asked, immediately shifting into crisis
management mode.

"Bad." Lyra didn't look up from her monitoring spells. "Whatever happened when you two were separated didn't just affect the
Observatory. The binding appears to be tied into the campus's
fundamental magical infrastructure somehow."

Through my connection with Ivy, I felt her horror at the implications. The binding wasn't just making us magically dependent on each other, it was making the entire university magically dependent on our proximity.

"That's impossible," I said, though even as the words left my mouth, I was remembering fragments of Blackthorn family lore that suggested it wasn't impossible at all. Ancient bindings weren't just about two people. They were about power, territory, and magical dominion over entire regions.

"Is it?" Lyra's pale eyes fixed on me with unsettling intensity. "The Winter Court laid the campus lattice. If the lattice recognizes this binding as legitimate authority..."

My stomach dropped. Of course. NPU had been built with Winter Court magic, designed to be a neutral ground where different supernatural communities could coexist and learn. But neutral didn't mean independent. The university's magical infrastructure was still ultimately tied to the court system that had created it.

And if someone had used an ancient Blackthorn binding to connect Ivy and me to that infrastructure...

"Someone isn't trying to control just us," I realized aloud. "They're testing control of the university through us."

"Through us," Ivy whispered, her face going pale as the scope of the manipulation became clear.

Dylan was already moving, his fox-shifter instincts sharp with protective anger. "Can we break the connection to the infrastructure without breaking your binding?"

"I don't know," Lyra admitted. "But we need to stabilize the immediate crisis first. The longer the magical chaos continues, the more risk there is of permanent damage to the campus systems."

She gestured to her displays, where the readings were deteriorating steadily. "The aurora patterns are destabilizing. The residential heating systems are fluctuating. Even the dining hall's food preservation spells are starting to fail."

Through our bond, I felt Ivy's growing panic. This wasn't just about us anymore, it was about every student on campus, every professor, every magical creature that called NPU home. If the infrastructure were to collapse entirely, hundreds of people could be hurt or worse.

"What do we need to do?" she asked, her voice steady despite the fear I could sense underneath.

"Get closer to each other," Lyra said immediately. "Physical proximity seems to stabilize the binding, which should help with the infrastructure fluctuations. But we also need to understand why separation causes such dramatic effects."

I moved to stand beside Ivy, and the moment I was within arm's reach, both our binding runes settled into that synchronized rhythm I was beginning to recognize. Through the Observatory's crystal walls, we could see the campus emergency lights beginning to dim as whatever crisis we'd triggered started to resolve.

But something else happened when our magic aligned. The nightmare frost that had been growing stronger , the twisted, hungry ice that was my family curse made manifest, quieted to a whisper. For the first time in months, my storm magic felt... peaceful. Controlled not through force or rigid discipline, but through harmony.

I wasn't ready for how much I wanted to keep that feeling. Want wasn't a luxury Blackthorns were allowed. I wanted anyway.

Ivy's presence didn't banish the darkness in my magical core. It gave it form, purpose, beauty. Like she was teaching my winter magic to remember what it had been before the curse twisted it into something destructive.

I'd never experienced anything like it. Never imagined that the chaotic ice storms in my chest could settle into something that felt like home.

"Better," Dylan observed, checking Lyra's readings. "The power fluctuations are stabilizing."

"But this is only a temporary fix," Lyra warned. "You can't spend every moment of the semester within..."

She stopped mid-sentence as Ivy shifted position, moving just a few steps away to get a better view of the monitoring displays. The moment the distance between us increased beyond five feet, both our binding runes flared with warning light.

The effect was immediate and dramatic. The Observatory's crystal walls vibrated with sympathetic resonance. Lyra's monitoring equipment spiked into the dangerous zone. Through the transparent dome above us, we could see the aurora patterns beginning to fracture again.

"Ivy!" I called, and she immediately stepped back into range.

The chaos settled as quickly as it had erupted, but the demonstration had proved Lyra's hypothesis with uncomfortable clarity.

"Five feet," Dylan said grimly. "That appears to be your maximum safe distance."

"Call it the Five-Foot Rule until we learn more," Lyra said, tapping a note into her research console. "And a time threshold, fifteen to twenty minutes apart starts the spiral. I'll log both."

Lyra's voice went quiet. "Every moment of the semester."

The Observatory's main entrance chimed, and Professor Blitzen strode in with the kind of crackling electrical energy that made the very air hum with restrained power. The temperature in the room dropped several degrees from her presence alone, and I felt Ivy move closer to my side instinctively.

This wasn't the controlled authority of a professor managing classroom discipline. This was raw magical dominance from someone who could level buildings if sufficiently provoked.

"Mr. Blackthorn," she said, her silver hair literally sparking with contained lightning, her pale eyes sharp enough to cut glass. "Miss Snowfall. I understand you two are responsible for the magical chaos that just forced us to evacuate half the academic wing?"

"Not intentionally," I replied carefully.

"Intention is irrelevant; outcomes are policy." Professor Blitzen's voice could have frozen flame. "When the results include exploding potion labs and aurora storms severe enough to disrupt sleigh traffic."

"An ancient binding with unexpected infrastructure connections," Lyra explained, her academic excitement barely contained despite the seriousness of the situation. "The magical signature suggests Winter Court origins, but the scope of effect is far beyond anything documented in partnership magic literature."

"Show me," Professor Blitzen commanded.

What followed was the most thorough and unsettling magical analysis I'd ever witnessed. Professor Blitzen's lightning magic interfaced with Lyra's research systems, creating detailed scans of both our individual magical signatures and the binding that connected us. Dylan provided historical context about partnership magic theory, while Ivy and I submitted to test after test designed to map the binding's effects.

Most of the scans were routine, magical density readings, compatibility assessments, bond strength measurements. But when Professor Blitzen attempted to analyze the binding's connection to NPU's infrastructure directly, something went wrong.

The moment her lightning magic touched the binding's deeper layers, both Ivy and I convulsed as if we'd been struck by actual electricity. The binding runes on our arms flared white-hot, and through our connection, I felt her pain as if it were my own, sharp, searing, and accompanied by the terrifying sensation that something fundamental in our magical cores was about to tear apart.

Her knees buckled; I caught her elbow, skin brushed skin; the burn halved. Contact stabilized the readings.

"Stop!" Lyra shouted, immediately cutting the analysis feed.

Professor Blitzen stepped back, her expression grim. "The binding has protective measures. Aggressive investigation triggers defensive responses."

Through our bond, I felt Ivy's lingering shock and the frightening realization that someone had designed this binding not just to control us, but to prevent anyone from understanding how to free us. Every layer of the magical construct was protected by increasingly dangerous deterrents.

"Are you both alright?" Dylan asked, moving closer with obvious concern.

"We're fine," I managed, though Ivy was trembling beside me and I wasn't feeling particularly steady myself.

The results of the less invasive tests were both fascinating and terrifying.

"The binding is definitely designed for territorial control," Professor Blitzen confirmed after reviewing the data. "Not just partnership magic, but dominion magic. The kind used to establish magical sovereignty over specific locations."

"Someone wanted to give us control over the university?" Ivy asked, confusion clear in her voice.

"Or they wanted to use your connection to seize control themselves," I said grimly. Through our bond, I felt her shiver as the implications sank in. "Create a binding tied to the infrastructure, then manipulate the bound parties to serve external interests."

"But why us specifically?" she pressed, and I felt her growing distress through our connection. "I'm nobody special. Just a sprite who barely passed Advanced Illumination last semester."

Through our bond, I caught flashes of her memories, three years of sitting in the back of lecture halls, avoiding professors' attention, deliberately dimming her magic to avoid standing out. She'd spent her entire academic career trying to be invisible, only to discover that someone had been watching her all along. Studying her. Planning for her.

The violation of that realization hit her like a physical blow. Her fingers tightened around the table edge; I felt the echo in my bones.

Professor Blitzen's expression grew thoughtful. "Miss Snowfall, what do you know about your family's magical lineage?"

"Not much," Ivy admitted, her voice smaller than usual. "My parents said we were descended from arctic sprites, but most sprite families have mixed heritage. Nothing particularly notable."

"And yet your light magic shows unusual resonance with winter elements," Professor Blitzen mused. "Almost as if it were designed to complement frost magic rather than oppose it."

Through our connection, I felt Ivy's growing unease deepen into something closer to fear. She'd never questioned why her magic was different from other sprites, but now that someone was examining it closely, the anomalies were becoming impossible to ignore. Had her parents lied to her about their heritage? Had they known she was different in ways that might attract dangerous attention?

"There's something else," Lyra added quietly. "The binding's magical signature suggests it was created specifically for your magical types. Not just any winter witch and any sprite, but winter magic with Blackthorn characteristics and light magic with arctic sprite heritage."

"A custom trap," Dylan realized. "Someone researched both your magical bloodlines and designed a binding that would only work with your specific combinations."

The implications hit me like a physical blow. This wasn't random political maneuvering or opportunistic manipulation. Someone had been planning this for years, possibly decades. Studying our families, analyzing our magical potential, waiting for the right moment to spring their trap.

"Who would have access to that kind of genealogical research?" I asked, though I was already afraid I knew the answer.

"The Winter Court keeps extensive records," Professor Blitzen confirmed. "Magical bloodlines, political alliances, potential threats to court stability. If someone wanted to identify two students whose binding could be used to control NPU's infrastructure..."

She didn't need to finish the thought. The Winter Court had the resources, the knowledge, and the political motivation to orchestrate exactly this kind of manipulation.

"Can we break it?" Ivy asked quietly.

"Not without significant risk to both of you," Professor Blitzen replied honestly. "Ancient dominion magic is designed to be permanent. Attempting to sever it could result in magical backlash severe enough to permanently damage your casting abilities."

"And the infrastructure connections?" Dylan pressed.

"Those might be modifiable," Lyra said thoughtfully. "If we can understand how the binding interfaces with the university's magical systems, we might be able to redirect or limit the connection without affecting the personal bond between Ivy and Rowan."

It wasn't the solution any of us had hoped for, but it was something.

"For now," Professor Blitzen continued, "you'll need to manage the proximity requirements carefully. I'll arrange for modified class schedules and dormitory assignments that minimize separation time."

"We're going to be together constantly," Ivy said, and I felt her mixture of anxiety and something that might have been anticipation through our bond.

"Is that... problematic?" Professor Blitzen asked, her sharp eyes noting the undercurrent of tension between us.

"No," I said quickly, before Ivy could voice any of the doubts I sensed from her. "We'll make it work."

Through our connection, I felt her surprise at my immediate acceptance, followed by a flutter of something warmer. Relief, maybe. Or gratitude that I wasn't going to make this situation more difficult than it already was.

"Good," Professor Blitzen nodded. "Because like it or not, you're partners now. Not just magically, but practically. Your academic success, your safety, and apparently the stability of our entire campus depend on your ability to work together."

As if to underscore her point, the binding runes on both our arms pulsed in perfect synchronization, and through the Observatory's crystal dome, we could see the aurora patterns above campus settling into the kind of beautiful, stable display that made NPU famous throughout the magical world.

"We'll figure it out," Ivy said quietly, and through our bond, I felt her determination strengthening. Not resignation, but resolve. The kind of quiet strength that had helped her survive three years at a university where she'd felt overlooked and underestimated.

"Yes," I agreed, looking at her properly for the first time since this crisis had begun. Really looking, seeing past the magical compatibility and political complications to the person who'd been thrown into this situation as unwillingly as I had.

She was small, yes. Unassuming in the way that had probably protected her from notice her entire life. But there was steel in her spine and fire in her pale eyes, and through our unwanted connection, I was beginning to understand that whoever had chosen her for this binding had underestimated exactly what kind of person they were trying to manipulate.

Which might be the first advantage we'd gained since this entire situation began.

I could work with underestimation. Underestimation was leverage. We needed it now.

"We'll figure it out together," I added, and meant it.

The binding rune pulsed once more, but this time it felt less like a leash and more like a lifeline.

Maybe that was progress.

CHAPTER FIVE
THE OBSERVATORY ARRANGEMENT

IVY

My new reality hit me at precisely six-thirty the next morning when a soft chime from my enchanted planner woke me with a message I'd never expected to receive:

Schedule Update: All classes have been relocated to the Observatory Annex. Partner proximity requirements in effect. Report to Lumina Wing by 7:00 AM for academic briefing. , Academic Affairs

I stared at the glowing text floating above my pillow, my sleep-addled brain struggling to process what this meant for my carefully structured life. No more slipping into lecture halls five minutes late and sitting in the back corner. No more avoiding group projects or optional study sessions. No more pretending I was just another unremarkable sprite working toward an unremarkable degree.

The binding rune on my wrist pulsed gently, as if sensing my mounting anxiety, and through our unwanted connection, I felt an echo of similar feelings from the bedroom next door. The connecting door between our rooms stood open, had been open all night, because closing it put too much distance between us. I could hear Rowan moving around in his space, the familiar sounds of someone trying to start their day quietly.

This is going to take some getting used to, his mental voice was clearer than it had been yesterday, the bond apparently strengthening overnight. The shared suite arrangements, I mean.

That's an understatement, I replied, then paused as I realized how easily the mental communication was becoming natural. *Are you... okay with this? The constant proximity thing? Living together?*

There was a moment of silence, and through the open doorway I could see his shadow pause on the wall. I caught the edge of something that might have been vulnerability before he replied. *Ask me again in a week. But for now... it's not the worst thing that could have happened.*

Which wasn't exactly a ringing endorsement, but considering we'd been magically bound against our will less than twenty-four hours ago, I supposed it could have been worse.

The Lumina Wing at seven AM was bustling with activity that clearly centered around our unusual situation. Professor Blitzen stood near the Observatory's main entrance, consulting with what appeared to be half the academic administration. Lyra moved between multiple research stations, her light magic dancing around crystalline displays that showed overnight readings from our binding. Dylan perched on a floating cushion nearby, offering commentary that somehow managed to be both helpful and irreverent.

"Ah, Miss Snowfall," Professor Blitzen said as I approached, her silver hair crackling with the residual electricity that seemed to follow her everywhere. "Punctual. Good. We have a great deal to arrange before your first modified class period."

"Modified how, exactly?" I asked, though I wasn't sure I wanted to know the answer.

"Your academic schedule has been restructured around partnership requirements," she explained with the kind of efficiency that suggested she'd been up most of the night making arrangements. "Classes will be held in spaces large enough to accommodate both you and Mr. Blackthorn without violating proximity limits. Professors have been briefed on the collaboration restrictions. Dormitory assignments have been... adjusted."

My stomach dropped. "Adjusted how?"

"Adjacent rooms with a connecting door," Dylan called from his floating cushion. "Don't panic...separate bedrooms, shared common area. Though based on last night's proximity readings, you might want to keep that connecting door open."

Through our bond, I felt Rowan's embarrassment matching my own as we both remembered how the first night had gone. We'd started out in separate rooms with the door closed, trying to maintain some semblance of privacy. That had lasted until 2 AM, when our binding runes had started pulsing with enough intensity to wake us both. He'd ended up pulling his mattress into the common area, close enough to my closed bedroom door that the runes finally settled.

Neither of us had gotten much sleep.

"It's actually a pretty sweet setup," Dylan continued, either oblivious to our discomfort or tactfully ignoring it. "Lyra and I consulted on the magical modifications. The suite can adapt as your proximity requirements shift."

Before I could fully process the implications of sharing living space with Rowan Blackthorn, and the memory of finding him asleep just outside my door this morning, the man himself arrived with the kind of perfectly controlled composure that made me wonder if he'd been awake for hours preparing for this conversation.

"Professor," he said with a respectful nod to Blitzen, then

caught my eye with something that might have been reassurance. "Ivy. How are you feeling about all this?"

Better now that you're here, I thought before I could stop myself, then felt heat creep up my neck as I realized he'd probably heard that.

Through our bond, I caught his brief surprise, followed by something warmer. *The proximity effects are definitely getting stronger.*

Is that what we're calling it?

For now.

Professor Blitzen cleared her throat with the authority of someone who'd noticed the silent communication and didn't have time for it. "As I was explaining to Miss Snowfall, your academic arrangements have been restructured. The Observatory Annex has been converted into a specialized classroom space. Your professors will rotate in rather than you rotating to different buildings."

"Like a magical house arrest," I muttered, then immediately regretted the comment when Professor Blitzen's pale eyes sharpened.

"Like a necessary accommodation," she corrected coolly. "Unless you'd prefer to explain to the families of three hundred other students why their children's education was disrupted by your binding's infrastructure connections."

The dismissal stung more than it should have. Three days ago, I would have accepted the rebuke and shrank back into invisibility. But something about being bound to Rowan, about suddenly mattering enough to disrupt an entire university, made me want to push back instead of fold.

I bit down on the impulse to point out that none of this was our choice, that we were victims of someone else's political game, not willing participants. Through our bond, I felt Rowan's mixture of approval for my restraint and understanding of my frustration.

"We'll make it work," Rowan said diplomatically.

Dylan bounced up from his cushion with characteristic enthusiasm.

"Now comes the fun part. The living arrangement needed some work so come see what we set up for you."

The "adjusted" dormitory space was located in the Lumina Wing's residential section, occupying what had apparently been a suite reserved for graduate researchers. Two bedrooms flanked a central common area that had been equipped with study stations, comfortable seating, and what appeared to be a fully functional magical kitchen.

The moment I stepped inside, I was struck by how thoroughly the space had been prepared. The air carried the crisp scent of pine wards and the subtle hum of protective enchantments woven into the walls. Crystalized warmth emanated from heating runes that had been carefully calibrated to accommodate different magical signatures. Even more telling, there was already a faint trace of frost along Rowan's assigned doorframe, his magic automatically marking territory even when he wasn't consciously casting.

"Privacy when you need it, proximity when the binding requires it," Dylan explained, gesturing around the space with obvious pride in the design. "Plus, you're only two floors down from the Observatory, so Lyra can monitor the binding's stability without having to trek across campus."

But as I took in the reality of what this meant, shared meals, shared study time, shared everything with someone I barely knew, my stomach clenched with anxiety that had nothing to do with magical binding.

"This is..." I started, then stopped. How did you politely say that moving in with a virtual stranger felt like too much, too fast, even when magical necessity demanded it?

Through our bond, I sensed Rowan's understanding of my discomfort, as well as his own uncertainty about the arrangement.

Awkward doesn't begin to cover it, his mental voice carried rueful honesty.

What if we can't stand each other by the end of the week? I thought back.

Then we'll figure out how to be miserable in close proximity without destroying the campus, he replied, and the dry humor in his tone made something ease in my chest.

I walked through what would apparently be my bedroom, larger than my previous dormitory room, with windows that looked out over the campus's snow-covered grounds and book-shelves that had already been stocked with my personal collection. Someone had clearly put significant effort into making this transition as comfortable as possible.

My own belongings had been similarly transported, my book-cases already stocked, my favorite blanket draped across the bed. Someone had even remembered my collection of pressed winter flowers, carefully arranged on the windowsill where morning light would catch them.

Across the common area, I could see Rowan moving through his own room with methodical precision, organizing belongings that had already been delivered while we were in our emergency briefing. Enchanted moving crates floated empty near the door, Dylan's handiwork, probably, while Rowan unpacked with the kind of careful control that suggested every placement was deliberate. Something was mesmerizing about the way he handled each item...books arranged by subject, magical implements organized according to some system I couldn't decipher, everything positioned exactly where it would be most useful.

You're staring, his amused mental voice interrupted my observation.

Heat flooded my cheeks as I realized he was right. *I was just... noting your system.*

I'll take that as a compliment, he thought back, then deliberately turned his attention to hanging up robes, giving me the privacy to process my embarrassment.

Which somehow made it more overwhelming rather than less.

"This is too much," I said quietly. "All this disruption, all these accommodations... for one binding that happened by accident."

"Not by accident," Rowan said from where he was examining his own room across the common area. "Remember? Someone planned this. Which means the disruption was always part of their strategy."

Through our bond, I felt his growing certainty about the political implications of our situation. He'd clearly spent time overnight thinking through the ramifications, and his conclusions weren't comforting.

"You think they wanted the university to accommodate us?" I asked.

"I think they wanted to see how far the university would go to avoid the chaos that separation causes," he replied, moving to lean against the doorframe between his room and the common area. "Every accommodation they make, every special arrangement, every exception to normal procedures, it all sets precedents. Every precedent sets a chain. And the Winter Court never leaves a chain unpulled."

Dylan's fox-shifter instincts had clearly picked up on the undercurrent of the conversation. "You're thinking this is a test case. See how much control the binding actually gives you over institutional decisions."

"It's what I would do," Rowan said grimly. "If I wanted to gradually establish magical authority over NPU without direct confrontation."

The implications of that settled over me like a cold weight. We weren't just bound to each other, we were bound to a political strategy that was larger and more complex than either of us had realized. Every choice we made, every accommodation we accepted, every precedent we set could be used to justify future manipulations.

"So what do we do?" I asked. "Refuse the arrangements? Insist on regular dormitories and classroom schedules even if it causes campus-wide chaos?"

"We play the game better than whoever set the rules," Rowan said, and through our bond, I felt his resolve crystallizing into something that might have been strategic planning. "They expected us to be puppets. We'll be partners instead."

Through our connection, I caught his brief surprise at how quickly he'd said that, followed by his realization that he meant it completely. He was noticing things about me, how my blush spread from my cheeks to my neck when embarrassed, how my magic automatically steadied his storm even when we weren't actively casting, how my spine straightened when I was trying not to back down from authority.

Partners. The word resonated through our connection in ways that had nothing to do with political maneuvering and everything to do with the growing awareness that we were stronger together than apart.

"Right now," Dylan interrupted with the cheerful pragmatism that seemed to be his specialty, "you need to focus on making it through your first day of modified classes without anyone realizing how much the binding has already changed since yesterday."

"Changed how?" I asked, though I suspected I already knew the answer.

"Your magical signatures are synchronizing faster than Lyra predicted," Dylan admitted. "The enhancement effects are getting stronger, and the proximity requirements are getting more specific. She thinks you might need to be within three feet of each other soon, instead of five."

Through our bond, I felt Rowan's mixture of concern and something else. Something that suggested the increasing proximity wasn't entirely unwelcome, which should have been more alarming than it was.

Are you worried about that? I asked him silently.

I'm worried about a lot of things, he replied honestly. *But not about spending time with you.*

The simple admission sent a flutter of warmth through me that had nothing to do with magical binding and everything to do with the growing realization that Rowan Blackthorn, notorious loner, Winter Court politics, cursed family magic, and all, was someone I was beginning to genuinely like.

Which was probably the most dangerous development in an already complicated situation.

"Ivy?" Dylan's voice interrupted my internal spiral. "You're broadcasting emotional resonance through the binding. Lyra's monitors are picking up some interesting readings."

I looked across the common area to where Rowan was watching me with an expression I couldn't quite read. Through our connection, I could feel his awareness of my growing attraction, along with his own confused response to it.

This is getting complicated, I thought at him.

It was already complicated, he replied. *The question is whether we're going to let it become complicated and impossible, or if we're going to figure out how to make it work.*

Before I could answer, the suite's communication system chimed with an announcement that our first modified class period would begin in fifteen minutes.

Time to find out if a magical partnership could survive Advanced Theoretical Applications when taught by a professor who'd probably never heard of proximity-dependent spellwork.

Together? Rowan's mental voice carried the kind of quiet determination that made my chest tighten with something that definitely wasn't just magical resonance.

Together, I agreed, and meant it.

The binding rune on my wrist pulsed once, as if acknowledging a decision that went deeper than magical accommodation.

Maybe Dylan was right. Maybe this was about more than politics or curses or the machinations of people who thought they could control our choices.

Maybe this was about discovering what happened when two people who'd never expected to find their place in the world suddenly realized they might have found it with each other.

CHAPTER SIX
TRIAL BY CLASSROOM

ROWAN

The Observatory Annex at eight in the morning looked like a cross between a lecture hall and a magical laboratory, with crystal displays along the walls and tiered seating fanning out in a semicircle around a central demonstration area. What it didn't look like was a normal classroom, and the dozen other students who'd been assigned to our modified Advanced Theoretical Applications section were clearly struggling to pretend otherwise.

Professor Meridian had been selective about the class composition, all partnership magic researchers or advanced theorists who'd signed comprehensive discretion agreements before even learning why they'd been reassigned. The administration had framed it as a "specialized experimental pedagogy section," not mentioning the binding that necessitated the modifications.

Still, I could feel their stares as Ivy and I took our seats at the specially positioned table. The proximity requirements were obvious to anyone paying attention, even if the specific reasons remained unclear. Some of the attention was academic curiosity, partnership magic theory was notoriously difficult to observe in practice. But Marcus Thornfield, a third-year ice mage and Ward Guild liaison, kept shooting us evaluative looks that suggested he was documenting every detail for official records. His whispered comment to his seatmate carried just far enough to reach us: "Fascinating case study in real-time magical dependency."

Through our bond, I felt Ivy's discomfort with the clinical scrutiny, along with her desperate wish to disappear back into the invisibility that had protected her for three years. Her fingers drummed against her desk in a nervous pattern that I was beginning to recognize, and without thinking, I shifted closer until our elbows almost touched.

The contact settled both our binding runes into that synchronized rhythm, and I felt her anxiety ease slightly.

Better? I asked through our mental connection.

A little, she replied, then caught herself staring at the other students. *They're all wondering what makes us so special that we get our own classroom setup.*

They're wondering what makes us so dangerous that we can't be trusted in regular classrooms, I corrected. Through the bond, I felt her surprise at the distinction, followed by her realization that I was probably right.

The difference mattered. Special treatment suggested privilege, favoritism, and advantages we hadn't earned. Containment suggested a problem to be managed. And while neither was entirely accurate, containment was closer to the truth.

Professor Meridian arrived with the kind of brisk efficiency that suggested she'd been briefed thoroughly on our unusual situation. She was a wind sprite herself, though her mastery of air magic far exceeded anything Ivy had achieved with light, and her pale green eyes took in our seating arrangement with professional interest rather than concern.

"Good morning, everyone," she said, her voice carrying the crisp authority of someone who'd been teaching advanced magical theory for longer than most of us had been alive. "Today we'll be working on stabilization techniques for mixed-element constructs. As some of you know, collaborative magic requires precise balance between different magical signatures to avoid dangerous resonance effects."

Her gaze lingered on Ivy and me for a moment longer than the others, but not unkindly. "Miss Snowfall, Mr. Blackthorn, given your current binding situation, you'll be working together throughout the exercise. The rest of you will be partnered randomly."

A few students exchanged glances that suggested they thought our "partnership" gave us an unfair advantage. Through our bond, I felt Ivy's flash of irritation at the assumption, followed by her determination to prove that whatever advantages we had, we'd earned them.

"The exercise is straightforward," Professor Meridian continued, gesturing to create a holographic display showing theoretical magical constructs. "Create a basic defensive ward using two different elemental approaches. Light and shadow, fire and water, air and earth, any combination that demonstrates your understanding of oppositional balance."

Around the room, students began pairing off and discussing strategies. The conversations were exactly what I'd expected, careful planning, measured magical output, conservative approaches designed to complete the assignment without drawing attention.

Ivy and I looked at each other, both thinking the same thing.

We should probably aim for understated, she said through our bond.

Probably, I agreed. *Simple light construct with frost reinforcement. Basic ward, nothing fancy.*

Right. Basic.

But the moment we began to channel our magic together, I knew "basic" wasn't going to be an option.

Ivy's light magic flowed from her hands in patterns that should have been familiar, standard illumination techniques, structured and controlled. But with my frost magic responding to hers through the binding, her constructs took on depths and complexities I'd never seen from sprite magic before. Instead of simple radiance, she was creating layered illumination that seemed to contain entire galaxies of light within each strand.

My frost magic, usually sharp-edged and aggressive, curved around her light constructs like liquid silver, reinforcing and enhancing rather than competing. The defensive ward that emerged from our combined efforts wasn't just functional, it was like the first barrier they created, beautiful, a shimmering barrier that looked like captured aurora, strong enough to stop a charging reindeer and lovely enough to hang in an art gallery.

The classroom had gone completely silent.

"Fascinating," Professor Meridian breathed, moving closer to examine our work. "The magical density readings are extraordinary, but more importantly, the balance is perfect. Most mixed-element constructs show stress fractures where different magics interface. This shows none."

Through our bond, I felt Ivy's mixture of pride and panic. We'd succeeded at the assignment beyond any reasonable expectation, but in doing so, we'd drawn exactly the kind of attention we'd been hoping to avoid.

"How are you achieving such seamless integration?" Professor Meridian asked, her professional curiosity clearly overriding any concerns about putting us on the spot.

"It's the binding," Ivy said quietly. "Our magical signatures synchronize automatically."

"But synchronization usually creates amplification, not integration," one of our classmates pointed out. "Your magic isn't just getting stronger, it's becoming something completely different."

Which was exactly what I'd been afraid someone would notice. Through our bond, I felt Ivy's growing realization that we were revealing more about our situation than might be wise.

"Different how?" Professor Meridian pressed.

I could have deflected, made some comment about partnership magic theory being beyond the scope of the current assignment. Should have deflected. But looking at the ward we'd created, at the way our magic had transformed simple techniques into something that belonged in advanced graduate research, I found myself answering honestly.

"Our individual magics complement each other in ways that exceed normal partnership effects," I said. "Ivy's light doesn't just work with my frost, it teaches my frost how to be constructive instead of destructive."

The moment the words left my mouth, I realized I'd revealed more than a magical technique. I'd revealed something personal, something that went to the heart of what the Blackthorn curse had done to my magic over the years. For a brief moment, I could see myself: twelve years old, at practice, hitting targets that splintered under ice that had gone hungry overnight, my tutor pale with the realization that something in me had turned.

I felt Ivy's sharp attention, along with her growing understanding that this was the first time I'd admitted out loud how much our partnership was changing my magical core.

"And your frost magic provides structure for her light constructs in ways that enhance rather than constrain," Professor

Meridian observed, her academic excitement growing. "This is remarkable work. Truly exceptional."

Exceptional. The word hung in the air like a promise and a threat. Exceptional students attracted attention. Exceptional magical phenomena attracted research interest. Exceptional partnerships connected to ancient bindings drew the interest of individuals specializing in political manipulation.

As if summoned by my growing concern, I felt a pulse from the binding rune on my ribs, not painful, but insistent. Like it was responding to something I hadn't noticed yet.

Rowan? Ivy's mental voice carried worry. *Your magic just spiked. What's wrong?*

I scanned the classroom, looking for whatever had triggered my instinctive wariness. Students were cleaning up from the exercise, packing away materials, and engaging in the kind of casual chatter that followed successful coursework. Professor Meridian was making notes on her assessment tablet, probably documenting our ward construction for future reference.

Everything looked normal. Felt normal.

Except for the leather satchel beside my chair, which definitely hadn't been there when class began.

Someone left something for me, I told Ivy through our bond, not wanting to alarm her unnecessarily but unable to shake the feeling that whatever was in that satchel wasn't a friendly gesture.

Left what?

I don't know yet.

As the other students filed out, chattering about assignments and upcoming examinations, I reached for the satchel with careful fingers. The leather was high quality, unmarked except for a small symbol embossed near the clasp, three interlocking snowflakes arranged in a triangle.

The Winter Court seal.

I heard Ivy's sharp intake of breath as she recognized the symbol's significance. *What do they want?*

Only one way to find out.

Inside the satchel was a single piece of parchment, folded with the kind of precise edges that suggested official correspondence. The message was brief, written in the flowing script favored by court scribes:

Mr. Blackthorn,

Your recent academic arrangements have been noted with interest. It appears the binding is proceeding exactly as intended. Your cooperation in maintaining current proximity parameters will be expected.

We look forward to observing your continued progress.

, A Friend

No signature, but the Winter Court seal was pressed into the parchment with the kind of magical binding that made the document impossible to forge.

They're watching us, Ivy said, her mental voice tight with the kind of fear that came from realizing you were a piece in a game whose rules you didn't understand.

They've been watching us since the beginning, I replied grimly. *This is just their way of letting us know they approve of how we're playing so far.*

Through our bond, I felt her mixture of anger and helplessness. We'd been managing our situation as well as we could, trying to balance magical necessity with personal autonomy, only to discover that our best efforts were apparently serving someone else's agenda perfectly.

What do we do?

We keep playing, I said, folding the parchment carefully and slipping it into my pocket. *But we play better than they expect us to.*

As we gathered our materials and prepared to leave the Observatory Annex, I caught Professor Meridian reaching into her desk drawer with the kind of deliberate casualness that suggested she'd been waiting for the right moment. When she looked up and met my eyes, there was that flicker of recognition again, concern sharpened into something like protective calculation.

Professor Meridian knows more than she's saying, Ivy observed through our bond.

Probably. The question is whether that makes her an ally or another complication.

The binding rune pulsed again as we walked toward the exit, and through the Observatory's crystal windows, I could see aurora patterns forming in the afternoon sky that definitely weren't natural.

Someone was sending messages. Multiple someones, if the different magical signatures in the light displays were any indication.

We weren't just students dealing with an inconvenient binding anymore. We were players in a political game that was growing more complex by the hour.

And based on the satisfaction I'd felt through that anonymous note, we were playing it exactly as someone had hoped we would.

The question was: how long before we figured out how to start playing for ourselves instead of for whoever was pulling the strings?

CHAPTER SEVEN

INVISIBLE NO MORE

IVY

The whispers started before I even entered the Crystal Dining Hall.

", only strong because of him..."

", heard she could barely light a candle before the binding..."

", typical sprite, piggybacking on real winter magic..."

I paused just outside the entrance, my appetite disappearing as the fragments of conversation reached me through the hall's acoustically enhanced architecture. Three years of careful invisibility, three years of flying under the radar and avoiding exactly this kind of attention, undone in a single spectacular classroom demonstration.

I felt Rowan's awareness of my distress, along with his own tightly controlled anger at what the other students were saying. He was somewhere behind me, close enough that the Five-Foot Rule was satisfied, but far enough back that I could pretend I was walking into this alone.

You don't have to pretend. His mental voice was gentler than usual. *We're partners, remember?*

Partners in making me the subject of campus gossip, I replied, then immediately regretted the bitter tone. *Sorry. That's not your fault.*

It's not yours either.

But it felt like my fault. Every whispered comment, every side-long glance, every conversation that stopped when I approached, it all felt like confirmation that I'd been right to stay invisible for so long. The moment I'd stepped into the light, people had started looking close enough to see exactly how small and unremarkable I really was.

I forced myself to walk into the dining hall with my chin up and my shoulders straight, the way I'd seen confident students do it. Undermined only by Rowan shadowing me at five feet, the most conspicuous invisibility attempt ever.

The Crystal Dining Hall sparkled with winter enchantments, from the chandeliers that cast rainbow patterns through suspended ice crystals to the soft chime of enchanted cutlery that adjusted temperature to keep hot foods steaming and cold foods crisp. The air carried the scent of peppermint cocoa and cinna-mon-spiced cider, creating a cozy warmth that contrasted with the nervous energy I felt radiating from nearby tables.

The dining hall buzzed with the kind of energy that came from three hundred students trying to talk around the most inter-esting gossip to hit campus in months. Tables of sprites clustered near the windows, their usual musical chatter replaced by pointed whispers. Ice magic students occupied their traditional corner, and I could feel their analytical gazes tracking our progress across the room.

"Ivy!" called a familiar voice, and I turned to see Petal Brightwood waving from a table near the dessert station. She was a fellow sprite, though her flower magic had always been more advanced than my light constructs. We'd been study partners occasionally, more out of convenience than friendship, but right now her smile looked genuinely welcoming.

I made my way over to her table, aware that Rowan was following and that every step we took was being catalogued by interested observers.

"How are you handling all this?" Petal asked as I slid into the chair across from her. "The binding, the modified classes, having to stay close to..." She glanced at Rowan, who had positioned himself at the adjacent table, giving us the illusion of privacy. There was something in her expression I hadn't noticed before, a flicker of envy, maybe, at the kind of attention that made professors restructure entire academic programs.

"We're managing," I said carefully.

"I heard your ward display in Professor Meridian's class was incredible," Willow Fernspike added from down the table, though her smile seemed a little forced. "Aurora-level magical density?"

Willow's fingers drummed against her cup in a pattern I recognized, the same nervous energy I got when other students accomplished things I thought should have been beyond their level. She'd been working on advanced constructs since her first year, and here I was accidentally creating graduate-level magic with someone I'd met three days ago.

"The professor said it was well-executed," I replied, trying to deflect without outright lying.

"Well-executed?" Petal laughed. "According to Marcus Thornfield, it was the most beautiful defensive construct he's ever seen. And he's been studying advanced ward theory since his first year."

Marcus had been one of the students shooting resentful looks our way during class, but apparently, his complaints about special treatment didn't extend to denying the quality of our work.

"It's the binding," I said quietly. "Our magic syncs automatically. It's not really... replicable? Preferably never in front of a hundred witnesses again?"

"Not really what?" Willow interrupted. "Not really your contribution? Ivy, you do realize that magical syncing doesn't happen unless both partners are contributing equally, right? If your magic was weak or incompatible, the binding would either fail completely or amplify his frost magic while leaving yours unchanged."

I hadn't known that. I could feel Rowan's agreement with Willow's assessment, along with his frustration that I was still doubting my own contributions to our partnership.

She's right, he said through our mental connection. *The enhancement effects work both ways. Your magic isn't piggybacking, it's providing the foundation for mine to become something better.*

Before I could respond, another voice cut through the dining hall's ambient noise with enough clarity to reach half the room.

"I suppose we'll never know what she was capable of on her own, will we?"

The comment came from Frost Silverleaf, a senior ice sprite whose family connections and natural talent had made her something of a celebrity among the winter magic students. She wasn't looking directly at me, but her voice carried the kind of casual authority that made nearby conversations pause. I noticed the lapel pin on her robes, three interlocking snowflakes in a triangle, catching the chandelier light.

"After all," Frost continued, ostensibly talking to her tablemates but clearly performing for a wider audience, "when someone's magical abilities undergo such dramatic enhancement after a binding, it does raise questions about their baseline competency."

The words hit like physical blows. Not because they were particularly cruel, but because they articulated the fear I'd been carrying since yesterday's demonstration, that everyone would assume my enhanced abilities meant my natural ones were negligible.

"Baseline competency compared to what metric?" I asked, my voice steadier than I felt.

Frost's eyebrows rose with the kind of surprise that suggested she hadn't expected me to respond directly. "Compared to established achievement patterns for your year and specialization, obviously."

"I'm the same caster I was yesterday," I said. "The binding didn't give me a new language, it gave me a better microphone."

I felt Rowan's approval of my response, along with his sharp anger at Frost's provocation. But before anyone could respond to my defense, another voice spoke up.

"Actually," Professor Meridian said, interrupting the conversation. "Miss Snowfall's baseline magical signature has been documented since her first year. Her light constructs showed unusual structural complexity even when working independently."

I hadn't noticed the professor entering the dining hall, but she was standing just behind Frost's table with a cup of tea and an expression that suggested she'd heard the entire exchange. A subtle draft followed her movement, making nearby napkins flutter despite the absence of any actual breeze, a telltale sign of wind sprite magic responding to emotional state.

"Her binding enhancement patterns indicate that she was providing architectural support for Mr. Blackthorn's frost magic from the moment their signatures synchronized," Professor Meridian continued. "That level of instinctive magical integration doesn't occur unless both partners possess complementary strengths."

As she spoke, her pale green eyes found mine across the room, holding my gaze for just a moment longer than casual interest would warrant. In that brief contact, I caught something that felt like recognition, not of me personally, but of something about our situation that she understood better than she was letting on.

The dining hall had gone suspiciously quiet. Even students at the far tables were straining to hear a professor's impromptu lecture on partnership magic theory.

"Furthermore," Professor Meridian added, her pale green eyes fixing on Frost with the kind of look that had probably withered decades of overconfident students, "suggesting that a bound partner's contributions are somehow less valid demonstrates a fundamental misunderstanding of how collaborative magic functions."

Frost's cheeks flushed pink, but she lifted her chin with the kind of defiance that came from never having been seriously challenged by authority. "I'm simply observing that dramatic enhancement raises questions about original capability. It's a reasonable academic inquiry."

"Is it?" Rowan's voice cut through the tension like a blade through silk. He'd risen from his position at the adjacent table and moved to stand behind my chair, close enough to feel his heat even without the rune. "Because from where I'm sitting, the only questions being raised are about why someone would feel the need to diminish another student's contributions when those contributions can be objectively measured and verified."

He wasn't shouting. Wasn't even raising his voice. But there was something in his tone, a cold, controlled authority that reminded everyone in the room that he was a Blackthorn, Winter

Court nobility, someone who'd been trained from childhood to navigate political confrontations.

Professor Meridian's response was swift and precise. "Then inquire reasonably. In a lab." She gestured casually toward Frost. "Miss Silverleaf, I'll expect a mixed-element ward replication study by Friday, source notes attached. Since you're so interested in baseline comparisons."

Frost's expression shifted from defiant to alarmed as she realized she'd just been assigned what amounted to a graduate-level independent study as a consequence for her public commentary.

Professor Meridian nodded approvingly and continued on her way to the faculty seating area, but not before making one more pointed observation: "I trust this kind of disruption during meal periods won't become a pattern. The dining hall is meant for nourishment, not academic theater."

The warning was gentle but clear, future confrontations would be met with administrative intervention. The dining hall was left to buzz with renewed conversation about what they'd just witnessed, though the volume remained more subdued than before.

I sat in my chair, staring down at my hands, trying to process the fact that I'd just been publicly defended by both a professor and a Winter Court heir. Three days ago, most of these students wouldn't have known my name. Now I had people arguing about my magical competency in front of half the campus.

Are you alright? Rowan asked through our bond as he settled back into his position at the adjacent table.

I don't know, I admitted. *This is all so strange. People talking about me, professors defending me, you coming to my aid...*

You defended yourself first, he pointed out. *I just provided backup.*

I didn't defend myself. I just sat there.

You stayed calm when someone was trying to provoke you. You didn't shrink back or apologize for being visible. That's its own kind of defense.

Through our connection, I caught an echo of his memories, court functions where political opponents had tried to bait him into reactions that could be used against him later, lessons in maintaining composure under pressure, and the understanding that sometimes the strongest response was refusing to give someone the reaction they wanted.

Is that what she was doing? Trying to provoke me?

Frost's family has connections to several Winter Court factions, Rowan replied grimly. *It's possible she was testing your reactions for someone else's benefit.*

The thought sent a chill down my spine that had nothing to do with the dining hall's temperature. Political manipulation was supposed to be something that happened to other people, important people, people with family names and magical legacies worth targeting.

You think someone told her to say that?

I think someone's been watching our situation closely enough to identify potential pressure points, he said. *Your confidence in your own abilities would be an obvious target.*

As if summoned by our conversation, my binding rune began to pulse with the familiar warning that meant we'd been apart too long. But Rowan was sitting less than five feet away, well within our established proximity limits.

Rowan, I said through our bond, not wanting to alarm the dining hall full of students who were already paying too much attention to us. *Something's wrong with the binding.*

I felt his instant alertness, followed by his own realization that his rune was pulsing in the same urgent rhythm. Around us, conversations began to quiet as students noticed the soft silver-white light emanating from both our arms, accompanied by a sound like distant wind chimes that seemed to come from the runes themselves.

"Are they supposed to do that?" someone whispered.

The pulsing intensified, shifting from silver-white to an urgent aurora-green, and suddenly I felt a desperate need to be closer to Rowan. Not just within five feet, within touching distance. The sensation was like being pulled by an invisible magnet, accompanied by a pins-and-needles feeling that spread from the rune up my entire arm.

The proximity requirements are tightening, he said. *Dylan warned us this might happen.*

How much closer?

Close enough that separate tables aren't going to work anymore.

The binding runes flared brighter, and this time the pull was impossible to ignore. I stood up from my chair just as Rowan rose from his, and we moved toward each other with the kind of synchronized motion that suggested our magical signatures were overriding our conscious decisions.

The moment our hands touched, the urgent pulsing settled into the familiar synchronized rhythm, and the desperate reaching sensation disappeared. But something else happened too, a subtle warmth where his cool palm met mine, accompanied by the faintest crackle of static where our different magics interfaced. Our breathing automatically synchronized, and for a heartbeat, the dining hall's noise faded to background whisper.

Our plates scooted toward each other across the enchanted table like they, too, had proximity requirements.

But we were now standing in the middle of the Crystal Dining Hall, holding hands, surrounded by three hundred students who were witnessing our latest magical development with expressions ranging from fascination to concern to barely disguised glee at having fresh gossip material.

Well, Rowan said through our bond, his mental voice carrying rueful humor. *I don't think we can pretend this is temporary much longer.*

How close do you think we'll need to be eventually? I asked, dreading the answer.

I'm trying not to think about that right now.

Through our joined hands, I could feel his steady presence, the way his magic instinctively adjusted to support mine, the growing familiarity of sharing headspace with someone whose thoughts were becoming as natural as my own.

The binding rune pulsed once more, gently this time, as if acknowledging that we'd accepted this new development.

Around us, the dining hall continued to buzz with excited whispers about what they'd just witnessed, but for the first time since this whole situation began, I found I didn't care as much about the attention.

Let them whisper. Let them speculate. Let them wonder what it meant that Ivy Snowfall, smallest sprite on campus, barely-passing student, former master of invisibility, was bound to someone who defended her publicly and held her hand like it was the most natural thing in the world.

Maybe I was finally ready to find out what it felt like to be seen.

A soft chime drew my attention to a message crystal that had appeared on our joined hands, glowing with official university formatting. The text materialized in floating letters:

Administrative Notice: Proximity parameter revision under review. Report to Observatory for controlled assessment at 1800 hours. , Academic Affairs

I felt Rowan's tension through our bond as he read the message. Whatever was coming next, it would be official, documented, and likely more intensive than anything we'd experienced so far.

Controlled assessment, I thought to him. *That sounds ominous.*

Everything about this situation has been ominous, he replied. *At least now we know they're taking it seriously.*

The message crystal dissolved, leaving only the faintest trace of administrative magic and the certainty that our relatively quiet period of adjustment was about to end.

CHAPTER EIGHT
CHAINS AND CHOICES

ROWAN

The summons came an hour before our scheduled "controlled assessment," delivered by a frost raven that materialized in our shared common room with the kind of magical signature that meant serious business.

Mr. Blackthorn. My office. Immediately. Come alone. , Professor Blitzen

I could feel Ivy's spike of anxiety as she read the message over my shoulder. The Three-Foot Rule meant we'd been together constantly since the dining hall incident, and the idea of separation, even for a faculty meeting, had both our binding runes humming with low-level warning.

How long can you be apart before it becomes a problem? I asked through our mental connection, though I was already dreading the answer.

I don't know, she admitted. *Yesterday we managed fifteen minutes. But the requirements keep tightening.*

I'll make it quick.

Professor Blitzen's office occupied a corner of the Administrative Tower, its walls lined with storm crystals that crackled with contained lightning and certificates of achievement that spoke to decades of academic excellence. She was standing behind her desk when I entered, her silver hair sparking with the kind of electrical energy that suggested whatever conversation we were about to have wasn't social.

The door sealed behind me, and the rune again reminded me of how long I've been away from Ivy. I had kept notes in my head as I walked over. Minute eight: a static itch under the ribs. Minute eleven: pins and needles. Minute thirteen: a thin, cold wire tightening through my sternum. I kept my face polite. Ivy didn't need my panic echoing through the bond.

"Sit," she commanded, gesturing to the chair across from her desk. "We need to discuss your situation frankly, and I prefer to do so without an audience."

I remained standing. "If this is about the proximity requirements..."

"This is about the Winter Court's interest in your proximity requirements," she cut me off. "And what that interest is likely to cost you if current trends continue."

The words hit me like a physical blow. I'd known the Court was watching, monitoring, and possibly manipulating our situation. But hearing it acknowledged by faculty made the political implications feel suddenly, devastatingly real.

"You've received contact from them," Professor Blitzen continued. It wasn't a question.

"Anonymous correspondence," I admitted. "Nothing that constituted a direct threat."

"Yet." Her pale eyes studied me with the kind of intensity that made me feel like a lightning rod in a storm. "Mr. Blackthorn, I'm going to tell you something that should probably remain confidential, but given the circumstances, I believe you need to understand what you're facing."

She activated a privacy ward with a gesture, the air around us shimmering with magical shields that would prevent eavesdropping or magical surveillance. I noticed that the hardware was etched with interlocking snowflakes, evidence of Winter Court provenance. Even here, their influence ran deeper than I'd realized.

"North Pole University exists on Winter Court land by arrangement, not by right," she said bluntly. "Our charter grants us academic independence, but it doesn't grant us sovereignty. If the Court decides that your binding represents a threat to their interests, they can revoke our protection."

My stomach dropped. "Meaning?"

"Meaning they can demand your extradition to face Winter Court justice for whatever charges they choose to bring. Magical malfeasance. Breach of bloodline obligations. Unauthorized use of dominion magic." Her voice carried the weight of someone who'd seen political maneuvering destroy promising students before. "The specific charges matter less than the precedent."

By minute fourteen, the cold wire in my sternum had become a knife. Through our bond, I felt Ivy's growing distress as our separation time extended, and I could sense her fighting not to seek me out despite the letter's explicit instructions to come alone.

"What do you recommend?" I asked, though I was afraid I already knew the answer.

"Leave," Professor Blitzen said simply. "Both of you. Take a semester abroad somewhere beyond Winter Court jurisdiction. Let whatever political interest this binding has generated fade into old news."

"And if we refuse?"

"Then you accept that every choice you make, every magical development, every precedent you set will be scrutinized by people who have been playing political games since before your great-grandparents were born." She leaned forward, her expression serious. "They're not just watching you, Mr. Blackthorn. They're studying you. Learning how the binding responds to pressure, how far they can push before you break."

As I pocketed her warning, I felt the weight of it settle beside the anonymous satchel note from yesterday. Same threat, new wrapping. The Winter Court's patience might be vast, but it wasn't infinite.

The binding rune flared against my ribs, hot and insistent, and I felt Ivy's panic spike through our connection. Whatever our current separation limit was, we'd reached it.

"I need to go," I said, already moving toward the door.

"Mr. Blackthorn." Professor Blitzen's voice stopped me at the threshold. "If the Winter Court comes for you, NPU can't shield you forever. Remember that."

I made it back to our suite in under five minutes, but it was already too late. I found Ivy curled in the corner of our common room, her arms wrapped around herself as waves of magical distress radiated from her binding rune. The moment I crossed the threshold, she looked up with eyes that were wide with the kind of fear that came from feeling fundamentally disconnected from your own magical core.

"It's alright," I said, crossing to her immediately and dropping to one knee beside her chair. "I'm here."

The moment our hands touched, the chaotic energy settled, but I could feel through our bond how much the separation had cost her. Not just discomfort, actual pain, like someone had been slowly tearing her magical signature apart.

That was awful, she said through our mental connection, her thoughts shaky with residual distress. *I felt like I was dissolving.*

I'm sorry. Blitzen wanted to discuss the political implications privately.

Bad news?

The kind that makes our current problems look simple.

But before I could explain what Professor Blitzen had told me, our shared communication system chimed with the reminder that our controlled assessment was scheduled to begin in twenty minutes.

The Observatory had been reconfigured for what looked like a comprehensive magical evaluation. Lyra's usual research stations had been supplemented with monitoring equipment I'd never seen before, crystalline arrays that hummed with analysis magic, containment fields that could probably stop a charging dragon, and enough faculty observers to suggest that whatever they were planning to test was considered both important and potentially dangerous.

Professor Blitzen arrived as we were examining the setup, her expression carefully neutral in a way that suggested our private conversation was now compartmentalized behind professional responsibility.

"The goal," she announced to the assembled faculty and observers, "is to map the binding's current parameters and establish safety protocols for future proximity requirements."

Dylan and Lyra exchanged glances that carried the weight of shared concern, but neither spoke up to question the methodology.

"We'll begin with standard separation tests," Professor Blitzen continued. "Gradual distance increases while monitoring magical stability. If distress occurs, the test will be immediately terminated."

What followed was the most systematic invasion of magical privacy I'd ever experienced. They separated us by inches, then feet, measuring the binding runes' responses with instruments that felt like they were dissecting our magical cores. Every pulse, every flare, every moment of discomfort was documented with clinical precision.

"Fascinating," murmured Professor Ember, the Department Head for Advanced Magical Studies. "The binding isn't just proximity-dependent, it's creating magical co-dependency. Their individual signatures are beginning to merge."

Through our bond, I felt Ivy's growing alarm at the implications of that observation. We weren't just bound together, we were apparently becoming magically incomplete without each other.

"Let's test the upper limits," Professor Ember suggested. "See how far we can push the separation before permanent effects occur."

That should have been my first warning that the assessment was moving beyond safe parameters. But I was too focused on monitoring Ivy's distress levels through our bond to recognize the danger until it was too late.

They separated us beyond the point of discomfort, beyond the point of pain, into territory that felt like magical amputation. Ivy's binding rune flared white-hot against her wrist, and through our connection, I felt her magical core beginning to fragment under the strain.

"Terminate," Ivy said, voice hoarse, eyes glassed with pain. She braced a palm against the console to stay upright. "This is a consent withdrawal. Terminate now."

"Stop," I said, my voice sharp with alarm. "You're hurting her."

"The readings are still within acceptable parameters,"

Professor Ember replied, his attention fixed on his monitoring instruments rather than on the student who was clearly in distress.

"That's sufficient, Professor Ember," Blitzen said, lightning gathering like a warning in her hair. He didn't look up. He should have.

"Stop," I repeated, and this time there was winter in my voice, the kind of cold authority that came from generations of Blackthorn political power.

But they didn't stop. If anything, Professor Ember seemed excited by the dramatic readings his instruments were providing, and he gestured for the technicians to increase the separation distance further.

That was when my control snapped.

The storm magic that had been building in my chest since the separation began erupted outward in a wave of frost and fury that had nothing to do with academic assessment and everything to do with someone threatening the person I was bound to. That I had sworn I would protect. The storm in me didn't spear; it veiled. Frost flowered from my outstretched hand in a sheet that webbed over consoles and cables, choking current, not throats. Glass screamed; no one bled.

"STOP!" I roared, and this time the word carried enough magical force to crack the Observatory's reinforced windows.

Professor Ember stumbled backward, his monitoring instruments sparking and failing as my storm magic interfaced violently with their delicate electronics. Around the room, faculty members activated defensive shields, but I wasn't attacking them, I was heading for Ivy, whose magical signature felt like it was dissolving entirely under the strain of forced separation.

I reached her just as she collapsed, her binding rune flickering like a dying candle. The moment our hands touched, the chaotic energy stabilized, but I could feel through our bond how much damage the test had done. Her magical core felt fractured, incomplete, like someone had torn away parts that were essential to her fundamental magical identity.

"That's enough," Dylan said, his voice cutting through the chaos with Fox-shifter authority. "The test is over."

Professor Meridian arrived with two wardens and a clipboard in hand. "Live-separation trials are suspended pending ethics review," she announced, voice cool as sleet. "Any further data collection occurs under my protocol or not at all."

"The readings were just reaching the critical threshold..." Professor Ember started to protest.

"The readings were about to cause permanent magical damage," Lyra interrupted, her light magic blazing as she moved to check Ivy's condition. "Look at her magical signature. Another thirty seconds and you could have severed the binding entirely."

"Data confirms a phase shift," Lyra continued, scanning the crystalline readouts. "You've left synchronization and entered interdependence. Safe separation without physical contact: ninety seconds. Safe distance with contact: two feet. Past that, degradation accelerates exponentially."

Through our connection, I felt Ivy's exhaustion and her growing realization that the faculty didn't fully understand what they were dealing with. They saw the binding as an academic curiosity to be studied, not as something that had become fundamental to our magical existence.

During the debrief, Lyra noted an intriguing detail: "I'm seeing anomalous resonance spikes when you share breath, close face-to-face proximity, versus simply holding hands. The data suggests your magical signatures harmonize more completely with increased intimacy."

Are you alright? I asked through our bond, though I could feel the answer was complicated.

I will be, she replied, but her mental voice was shaky with the aftereffects of magical trauma. *But Rowan, I don't think they realize how deep this goes. The binding isn't just changing our magic, it's changing us.*

I helped her to her feet, keeping our hands linked as the binding runes settled back into their synchronized rhythm. Around us, faculty members were examining their damaged equipment and exchanging concerned glances about what they'd just witnessed.

"Mr. Blackthorn," Professor Blitzen said quietly, her voice carrying none of the warmth it had held during our private conversation. "Perhaps you could explain what just happened to your magical control."

"Someone was threatening my partner," I said simply. "My magic responded accordingly."

The words hung in the air like a challenge. Not my academic partner, not my binding partner, not even my magical partner. Just my partner, with all the personal and protective implications that came with it.

Through our bond, I felt Ivy's surprise at my choice of words, followed by something warmer that felt like gratitude. The word lodged in her chest like a spark finding tinder. *Partner.*

"I see," Professor Blitzen said, and her tone suggested she understood more about the situation than she was letting on. "Well. I believe we have sufficient data for now."

As the faculty began to pack up their damaged monitoring equipment, Dylan approached us with the kind of casual concern that suggested he'd been expecting something like this to happen.

"How are you feeling?" he asked Ivy directly.

"Like someone tried to tear my magical core in half," she admitted. "But stable now."

"The binding is deeper than we initially thought," Lyra added, her academic voice carrying an undertone of worry. "The magical integration is approaching permanent levels. At this point, attempting to break the connection could cause irreversible damage to both your magical cores."

Permanent, I thought through our bond. *No going back.*

Did you want to go back? Ivy asked, and there was something vulnerable in her mental voice that made my chest tighten with emotions I wasn't ready to name.

No, I realized with surprise. *I don't think I do.*

Through our joined hands, I felt her relief, followed by her own tentative admission that permanent didn't sound as terrifying as it should have.

We were bound now in ways that went far beyond magical necessity. The question was whether we were ready to choose what that meant for both of our futures.

Looking at Professor Blitzen's concerned expression, Dylan's protective stance, and Lyra's worried calculations, I had the feeling that the question was going to be answered sooner than either of us was prepared for.

But as Ivy's fingers tightened around mine and our binding runes pulsed in perfect harmony, I realized that some choices made themselves.

We were partners. Everything else was just details.

Back in the suite, a thin envelope slid under the door, the wax seal cooling to mirror-bright silver. Three interlocked snowflakes, and, inset at the edge, a smaller sigil I recognized now: Silverleaf. *A formal notice of observation.* Ivy's fingers found mine without needing the rune to tell them to.

CHAPTER NINE
AURORA SECRETS

IVY

The recovery took three hours.

Three hours of Rowan's steady presence anchoring me while my magical core painfully reassembled itself from the fragments the faculty stress test had left behind. By the time the worst of the magical trauma faded, evening had settled over North Pole University like a soft blanket, and the aurora borealis was beginning its nightly dance across the campus sky.

"I need air," I said finally, flexing my fingers to test whether my light magic was responding normally again. "Real air, not recycled indoor atmosphere."

Through our bond, I felt Rowan's agreement, along with his own restless energy that came from hours of controlled sitting when every instinct had been screaming at him to do something more active to help with my recovery.

"Observatory deck?" he suggested.

The Observatory's upper platform had become our unofficial retreat over the past few days, close enough to Lyra's monitoring equipment to satisfy administrative concerns, private enough to have conversations without an audience, and high enough to provide the kind of perspective that made campus problems feel manageable.

We made our way up the crystalline staircase, maintaining the two-foot proximity that had become our new normal. The Silverleaf notice was tucked safely in Rowan's pocket, but I could feel his awareness of it through our bond, another layer of political complication that we'd deal with tomorrow.

Tonight, I just wanted to breathe.

The deck was empty when we arrived, wrapped in the kind of peaceful quiet that came with being above most of the campus activity. Through the transparent crystal barriers, we could see students moving between buildings, warm light spilling from dormitory windows, the gentle glow of enchanted pathways that kept the grounds navigable even in perpetual winter twilight.

But it was the aurora that drew my attention. Tonight's display was particularly spectacular, with ribbons of green and gold light dancing across the sky in patterns that seemed almost responsive to our presence. As we watched, the colors deepened and shifted, creating formations that looked less like natural phenomena and more like intentional artistry.

"It's beautiful," I said, settling onto one of the cushioned benches that lined the deck's perimeter.

"It's reacting to us," Rowan replied, taking his place beside me close enough that our shoulders touched. "Look at the way the patterns change when our magical signatures align."

He was right. Every time our binding runes pulsed in synchronization, the aurora responded with shifts in color and intensity that suggested our partnership was somehow interfacing with the university's ambient magic in ways we didn't fully understand.

"Lyra's going to want to study this," I said with a mixture of fascination and resignation.

"Probably. But not tonight." Through our bond, I felt his determination that we have at least a few hours of peace before diving back into the academic analysis of our situation. "Tonight, we just exist."

Just exist. When was the last time I'd done that? Three years of trying to be invisible, three years of carefully managing my magical output to avoid attracting attention, three years of existing in the spaces between other people's notice.

"Can I ask you something personal?" I said, the words coming out before I'd consciously decided to speak them.

"We're magically bound and sharing living space," Rowan replied with dry humor. "I think we're past worrying about personal boundaries."

"What was it like growing up knowing you'd inherit a curse?"

The question hung in the air between us, and through our bond, I felt his surprise at my directness. But there was something about the aurora's gentle light and the privacy of the deck that made difficult conversations feel possible.

"Lonely," he said finally. "From the time I was old enough to understand what the Blackthorn legacy meant, I knew I'd have to be careful about getting close to people. The curse doesn't just affect the person who carries it, it affects everyone around them."

Through our connection, I caught flashes of his childhood memories. A seven-year-old boy practicing magic alone because his frost spells had started turning destructive without warning. Tutors who taught him control techniques but maintained professional distance. Family gatherings where relatives watched him with the kind of wariness usually reserved for dangerous animals.

"I learned early that the safest thing for everyone was if I kept my distance," he continued. "Maintain control, don't form attachments, don't let anyone close enough to get hurt when the curse decided to assert itself."

"That sounds awful," I said quietly.

"It was practical," he replied, but I could feel through our bond that practical didn't mean it hadn't hurt. "What about you? What was it like growing up knowing your magic was different from other sprites?"

I hesitated, surprised by how much I wanted to answer honestly. "Confusing. Other sprite children could create light constructs that danced and played, and interacted with each other. Mine were always... serious. Structured. Like they were trying to build something instead of just being beautiful."

The memory came back with unexpected clarity, being eight years old at a family gathering, watching my cousins create a garden of luminous flowers that sang in harmony, while my contribution had been an intricate geometric pattern that had impressed the adults but left the other children looking puzzled.

"My parents said it was just a phase, that I'd grow into more typical sprite magic as I got older. But it never happened. If anything, my light became more architectural, more focused on creating frameworks rather than artwork." I paused, remembering our ward construction in Professor Meridian's class. "I think that's why our defensive ward worked so well. I wasn't trying to create art, I was building a foundation that your frost could turn into something beautiful."

"Like it was designed to support other magic instead of standing alone," Rowan observed.

"Exactly." I turned to look at him, noting how the aurora's glow caught the sharp angles of his face and made his pale eyes seem to hold their own inner light. "Did you ever wonder if the curse was the whole story? If maybe your magic was meant to work with someone else's from the beginning?"

Through our bond, I felt his sharp attention, along with his realization that he'd been wondering the same thing since our partnership began.

"The destructive phase always felt wrong," he admitted. "Like my frost magic was trying to reach for something that wasn't there, and when it couldn't find what it needed, it turned cruel instead."

"And now?"

"Now it feels like it found what it was looking for."

The simple admission sent warmth through our connection that had nothing to do with magic and everything to do with the growing understanding that whatever had brought us together went deeper than political manipulation or academic curiosity.

We sat in comfortable silence for a while, watching the aurora patterns shift and dance above us. But gradually, I became aware that the colors were forming shapes that looked almost familiar, not random light displays, but deliberate configurations that seemed to carry meaning.

"Rowan," I said softly, "are those supposed to look like symbols?"

He followed my gaze upward, and I felt his tension spike through our bond as he recognized what I was seeing.

The aurora had arranged itself into three distinct formations, each one hanging in the sky like a suspended sigil. They pulsed with rhythmic light that seemed to match the beating of our hearts, and as we watched, the symbols began to rotate slowly, as if displaying themselves for examination.

"Activation runes," Rowan said grimly. "The same patterns that were on the binding charm."

"What do they mean?"

"If I'm reading them correctly? Surveillance, control, and summoning." His voice carried the weight of someone who'd been forced to study Winter Court magical theory from child-hood. "Someone's not just watching us, they're preparing to take direct action."

"You think someone's about to trigger the second stage."

"I think someone's been waiting for us to reach exactly this level of magical integration before moving to the next phase of whatever they have planned."

The aurora patterns pulsed brighter, and I felt our binding runes respond with synchronized flares of light that seemed to acknowledge some kind of magical signal.

"Should we tell Dylan and Lyra?" I asked.

"We should," Rowan agreed. "But not tonight. Tonight, they appear to be sending a message that they want us to see, not responding to an immediate threat."

As if confirming his assessment, the sigils began to fade, dissolving back into ordinary aurora patterns that danced across the sky with natural randomness.

"Besides," he continued, "I think we need to understand what we mean to each other before we start dealing with what we mean to other people's political strategies."

The words hung between us with the weight of honest admis-sion. We were partners now in ways that went far beyond magical binding or academic accommodation. The question was whether we were ready to acknowledge what that partnership was becoming.

I turned to face him more directly, close enough that our breaths mingled in the cold air. Through our bond, I felt his awareness of the proximity, along with Lyra's observation about magical resonance spikes when we share breath.

"What do we mean to each other?" I asked quietly.

"I don't know yet," he replied, his voice equally soft. "But I know I don't want to find out from a distance."

The aurora pulsed gently overhead, and our binding runes responded with warm synchronization that felt like approval. Whatever was coming next, political complications, magical developments, or the simple challenge of figuring out how to be two people who'd found something unexpected in each other, we'd face it the way we'd faced everything else.

Together, close enough to share breath and dreams and whatever secrets the winter sky was writing above us.

For the first time since the binding charm had fused to my wrist, that felt like a choice instead of a compulsion. But even as warmth spread through me at the thought, a whisper of fear followed it. Choosing to care about someone meant choosing to be vulnerable to losing them. And with Winter Court politics closing in around us, that vulnerability felt dangerous in ways I wasn't ready to acknowledge.

And that, I realized, made all the difference, both the choosing and the risk that came with it.

CHAPTER TEN
UNWANTED AUDIENCE

ROWAN

The Winter Court envoys arrived during morning meal service, because nothing said "diplomatic observation" quite like disrupting three hundred students trying to eat breakfast.

I felt them before I saw them, a collective magical presence that made my binding rune pulse with recognition and my storm magic coil defensively in my chest. Through our bond, I felt Ivy's immediate tension as she picked up on my reaction, her light magic automatically responding to stabilize whatever threat my instincts had identified.

"Winter Court," I said quietly, not wanting to alarm the other students at nearby tables but needing her to understand why every protective instinct I possessed had just activated simultaneously.

The dining hall's main entrance shimmered with portal magic, and three figures stepped through with the kind of calculated elegance that announced their importance to anyone paying attention. They wore the formal ice-blue robes that marked them as official court representatives, and each carried themselves with the particular brand of authority that came from centuries of political experience.

I recognized the leader immediately, and my stomach dropped.

Lord Darian Frostborn. My father's younger brother. The man who'd been instrumental in engineering my exile from court politics after my parents' deaths. He moved through the dining hall with the confident stride of someone who owned whatever space he occupied, his pale eyes scanning the room until they found mine.

The smile he offered when our gazes met was polite, politically correct, and absolutely lethal.

"Nephew," he said as the envoy reached our table, his voice carrying just enough warmth to sound familial to anyone listening. "How delightful to see you looking so... settled."

Through our bond, I felt Ivy's spike of alarm as she realized this wasn't just a formal diplomatic visit. This was family business, which in Winter Court terms meant it was personal, political, and probably dangerous.

"Uncle," I replied with equal politeness, rising to perform the courtesy bow that court protocol demanded. "I wasn't aware the Winter Court had business at North Pole University."

"Observation mission," said the second envoy, a woman whose arctic beauty and razor-sharp smile marked her as someone accustomed to using appearance as a weapon. "We've heard such interesting reports about recent... developments in partnership magic."

Her gaze slid to Ivy with the kind of clinical assessment that made my protective instincts flare. Through our bond, I felt Ivy straighten her spine in response to the scrutiny, and I was reminded again that whatever else she was, she wasn't someone who backed down from challenges.

"Indeed," Lord Darian continued, settling into the chair across from us with the casual authority of someone who expected accommodation wherever he went. "The Winter Court has always taken an interest in magical innovations that affect our territorial concerns."

The third envoy remained standing, and something about his position and alertness suggested he was there for protection rather than diplomacy. Which meant they were expecting trouble, or planning to cause it.

"Partnership magic isn't exactly an innovation," Ivy said calmly, her voice carrying just enough edge to suggest she wasn't intimidated by royal relatives or court politics. "It's been documented for centuries."

I felt my admiration for her spike through our bond, along with my growing concern that she was about to become the target of whatever political game my uncle was playing.

"Ah, but documentation and practical application are very different things," the female envoy observed with the kind of smile that suggested she found Ivy's response charmingly naive. "Particularly when that application involves magical signatures with... unique hereditary implications."

"Lady Silverleaf," Lord Darian said by way of introduction, "may I present my nephew, Rowan Blackthorn, and his... partner, Miss Ivy Snowfall."

The way he paused before saying "partner" made it clear he was testing the label, seeing how we'd respond to having our relationship defined by someone else's political framework.

But it was the name Silverleaf that made my blood run cold. Lady Silverleaf. As in Frost Silverleaf's family, the same family whose sigil had been on the formal notice that had appeared under our door. The dining hall confrontation hadn't been random student drama, it had been reconnaissance.

Through our bond, I felt Ivy's sharp realization as she made the same connection.

"Lady Silverleaf," she said with perfect politeness. "I believe I've met your daughter. Charming girl."

The response was so diplomatically cutting that I had to suppress a smile. Whatever else Ivy had learned during her years of staying invisible, she'd apparently absorbed some lessons in academic politics along the way.

"Yes, Frost mentioned she'd had the opportunity to observe your... collaborative techniques," Lady Silverleaf replied smoothly. "Quite impressive, from what I understand."

"Standard ward construction," Ivy said dismissively. "Nothing that wouldn't be covered in any advanced partnership magic curriculum."

"If such a curriculum existed," Lord Darian interjected with casual authority. "Which, of course, it doesn't. Partnership magic has been considered too unstable for formal academic instruction for nearly two centuries."

The trap in his words was beautifully laid. Either we were practicing dangerous, unauthorized magic that should be stopped, or we were pioneering legitimate magical research that should be controlled. Either way, the Winter Court had grounds for intervention.

"Perhaps," said a new voice from behind the envoys, "that's an oversight the university should address."

I turned to see Professor Meridian approaching with the kind of calm determination that suggested she'd been monitoring this conversation and had decided it was time to intervene. Her wind sprite magic created a subtle atmospheric shift that made the envoys unconsciously step back, giving our table more breathing room.

"Lord Darian, Lady Silverleaf," she continued with professional courtesy. "I wasn't aware the Winter Court had scheduled an academic evaluation visit."

"Observation mission," Lord Darian corrected, his tone suggesting that the distinction was important. "We're simply here to witness the... developments that have been reported to us."

"How fortunate," Professor Meridian replied. "I'm sure you'll find our partnership magic research protocols quite thorough. All conducted under proper academic supervision, with full documentation and safety measures."

The polite verbal sparring might have continued indefinitely, but it was interrupted by Ivy doing something completely unexpected.

She stood up.

Not dramatically, not defiantly, just rose from her chair with the kind of quiet dignity that commanded attention from everyone at nearby tables. Through our bond, I felt her determination crystallizing into something that felt suspiciously like a strategic decision.

"Lord Darian," she said, addressing my uncle directly, "you mentioned territorial concerns. Perhaps you could clarify what specific Winter Court interests are affected by an academic binding between two students?"

The question was beautifully simple and absolutely dangerous. She was asking him to state his political objectives openly, in front of witnesses, in a way that would require him to either admit the Court was overreaching or provide legitimate justification for their interference.

I felt my admiration for her spike even higher, along with my terror that she was directly challenging someone who could destroy both our lives with a single political decision.

"An astute question," Lord Darian replied, his pale eyes studying Ivy with what might have been approval. "The Winter Court's interest lies in ensuring that magical developments within our sphere of influence don't create unintended consequences for regional stability."

"And you believe our binding creates instability?" Ivy pressed.

"I believe," Lady Silverleaf interjected smoothly, "that magical bonds with territorial implications require careful monitoring to ensure they serve appropriate purposes."

The words hung in the air like a barely veiled threat. They weren't just here to observe, they were here to evaluate whether our partnership served Winter Court interests, and if it didn't, to take steps to ensure that it did.

Through our bond, I felt Ivy's understanding of what we were facing, along with her growing anger at being treated like a political asset rather than a person with her own agency.

"Territorial implications," she repeated thoughtfully. "You mean the binding's interface with North Pole University's magical infrastructure."

"Among other things," Lord Darian confirmed.

"And if our binding were to develop in ways that didn't align with Winter Court interests?" Ivy asked with the kind of deceptive casualness that suggested she already knew the answer.

I felt a flutter of nerves beneath her confident exterior, the realization that she was about to challenge people who could destroy her life with a word. I steadied my own magical signature, letting calm flow through our connection to anchor her.

"Then adjustments would need to be made," Lady Silverleaf said with a smile that made my blood run cold.

The threat was now explicit. Comply with Winter Court

objectives, or face consequences that could range from political pressure to magical intervention to physical removal from the university.

But instead of backing down, Ivy did something that made every envoy at the table reassess her as a potential player rather than a pawn.

She smiled back.

"How interesting," she said pleasantly. "I wasn't aware the Winter Court had jurisdiction over individual magical development within academic institutions. Perhaps Professor Meridian could clarify the relevant legal frameworks?"

Professor Meridian's expression suggested she was enjoying this diplomatic chess match more than she probably should have been. "Academic magical development falls under university charter protections, unless Winter Court sovereignty is directly threatened. Which, of course, would require demonstration of specific harm to Court interests."

"Specific harm," Ivy mused. "Not potential harm. Not theoretical harm. Specific, documentable harm to Winter Court interests."

"That is correct," Professor Meridian confirmed.

I felt Ivy's satisfaction as she realized she'd just maneuvered the envoys into a position where they'd have to prove their case rather than simply asserting their authority.

Lord Darian's expression shifted from politely threatening to genuinely impressed. "You argue like someone with legal training, Miss Snowfall."

"I argue like someone who doesn't appreciate being threatened over breakfast," Ivy replied calmly.

The dining hall around us had gone suspiciously quiet as students at nearby tables realized they were witnessing what amounted to a formal diplomatic confrontation. Through our bond, I felt Ivy's awareness of the audience, along with her strategic decision to use their presence as protection.

"No threats have been made," Lady Silverleaf said smoothly. "Merely observations about the importance of... appropriate guidance for developing magical partnerships."

"Guidance," Ivy repeated. "From the Winter Court. For a binding that occurred without Winter Court involvement, between students who aren't Winter Court citizens, at an institution that operates under its own charter."

She was systematically dismantling their justification for interference, and I could see from Lord Darian's expression that he was beginning to realize he'd underestimated exactly what kind of person he was trying to manipulate.

"Miss Snowfall," he said with the kind of dangerous pleasantness that preceded political consequences, "you seem to be under the impression that Winter Court interest requires formal jurisdiction."

"Doesn't it?" Ivy asked innocently.

"The Winter Court protects its interests through whatever means prove... effective," Lady Silverleaf added with a smile that suggested those means weren't always limited to legal frameworks.

And there it was. The implicit threat that had been lurking beneath the diplomatic language. The Winter Court would take whatever action they deemed necessary, legal authority or not.

Through our bond, I felt Ivy's spike of fear, quickly followed by her determination not to show it. But I also felt something else, a kind of protective fury that rose in response to watching someone I cared about being threatened by my family's political machinations.

"Uncle," I said quietly, my voice carrying the kind of winter chill that reminded everyone present that I was a Blackthorn,

Winter Court nobility, and someone whose magical heritage ran just as deep as his, "I think you may be overestimating the Winter Court's influence at North Pole University."

His pale eyes fixed on me with sharp attention. "Am I?"

"Academic institutions have their own methods of protecting their interests," I replied, gesturing slightly toward Professor Meridian and the growing number of faculty members who had begun to gather at nearby tables. "Methods that don't always align with court politics."

"How unfortunate that would be," Lord Darian said pleasantly. "For everyone involved."

The threat was now completely explicit. The Winter Court was prepared to escalate this situation beyond diplomatic observation if their interests weren't accommodated.

But before anyone could respond, Lady Silverleaf reached into her robes and withdrew something that made my blood turn to ice in my veins.

A crystalline activation key, carved with intricate runes that matched the patterns we'd seen in last night's aurora display.

The moment I saw it, my storm magic reacted instinctively, not to an external threat, but to the promise of forced control. The curse that lived in my magical core had been born from exactly this kind of political manipulation, and every part of my inherited power trembled on the edge of defensive fury.

I could feel Ivy's terror as she realized what we were looking at, and I had to fight to keep my own magical signature from spiraling into the kind of destructive chaos that would give them an excuse to use whatever power that key contained.

"Fortunately," Lady Silverleaf said with a smile that was all predator and no warmth, "we came prepared to ensure that everyone's interests are properly... aligned."

The Winter Court hadn't come to observe our binding's development.

They'd come to control it.

The dining hall's temperature dropped several degrees as Professor Blitzen materialized near our table, her silver hair crackling with contained lightning and her presence radiating the kind of storm authority that made even Winter Court envoys pause. Her pale eyes took in the activation key, the political standoff, and the growing crowd of faculty witnesses with the calculation of someone who'd been monitoring the situation and had decided it was time to intervene directly.

"Lord Darian," she said pleasantly, electricity dancing between her fingers, "I trust you have proper documentation for bringing Winter Court artifacts onto university grounds?"

The question hung in the air like the promise of lightning, and I realized that whatever was about to happen next, it was going to be much bigger than a diplomatic breakfast conversation.

CHAPTER ELEVEN
FAULT LINES

IVY

The envoys didn't leave. They multiplied, at least, that's how it felt. Everywhere Rowan and I went, the Winter Court's pale attention followed like frost on glass. The library, the Observatory, even the casual student spaces that should have been neutral territory, Lord Darian appeared with the persistence of winter, taking notes with clinical detachment that made my skin crawl.

The proximity rule had shifted again overnight. "Within reach" had become constant contact, skin to skin, magical signature to magical signature, hearts beating in unconscious synchronization. We learned the choreography fast: sidestep through doorways together, trade hands to take notes, accept Petal's spare stylus when mine kept wobbling because I wouldn't risk breaking the circuit between us.

The rune purred when our fingers laced; it rasped the moment we tried to pretend we were normal.

"They're documenting everything," Rowan said through our

mental connection as we approached Advanced Theoretical Applications. His voice carried the tight control that had become familiar, anger compressed into ice, frustration transformed into strategy. "Every spell we cast together, every time the binding runes pulse, every moment of enhanced magical output."

For what purpose? I asked, though I was afraid I already knew the answer.

Evidence. Either that we're dangerous enough to require intervention, or useful enough to be worth controlling.

Professor Meridian's gaze flicked to our joined hands the instant we entered her classroom, her pale green eyes noting the constant contact with professional observation. Lady Silverleaf had positioned herself in the back corner with a crystalline tablet angled just so, hunter's posture disguised as academic interest.

"Today we'll be working with defensive constructs under stress conditions," Professor Meridian announced, gesturing to create a holographic display of theoretical ward structures. "Balance and adaptation under external pressure."

How appropriately meta, Rowan observed through our bond, dry as polar air.

"Partner assignments are as established," Professor Meridian continued, which meant Rowan and I would continue working together while other students paired off in traditional random combinations.

But as we took our position at the demonstration table, something felt different about the way our magical signatures were interfacing. Not just the constant physical contact or the awareness of being observed, something fundamental had shifted overnight.

"Try a basic illumination construct," Rowan suggested quietly. "Something simple while we figure out what's changed."

I called up my light magic, expecting the enhanced brightness that had become normal when our powers synchronized. Instead, I got something that made both of us freeze in surprise.

The light that bloomed from my palms wasn't just brighter, it was structured with geometric precision that belonged to frost magic rather than sprite illumination. Crystalline patterns that looked like frozen starlight, creating formations that were both beautiful and utterly foreign to everything I'd understood about my own magical signature.

"Angle the lattice six degrees," I said without thinking, my voice carrying the confidence of someone who understood structural magic at a fundamental level. "Light shear stabilizes along the frost spine."

I caught Professor Meridian's sharp look of respect, not surprise, but professional recognition of technical mastery that shouldn't have been possible for someone with my academic background.

"That's not sprite magic," Marcus Thornfield said from the next table over, his voice carrying a mixture of awe and concern. "That's architectural light."

His frost magic was responding to mine, but not in the familiar supportive way that had characterized our partnership so far. Instead, it felt like our magical cores were beginning to overlap, sharing techniques and capabilities that should have been impossible to transfer between different magical types.

"The binding is facilitating knowledge transfer," Professor Meridian said quietly, though her voice carried enough to reach other students who had stopped their own exercises to watch. "Amplification made your magic louder. Integration tuned you to the same key. This is different, blending. Your magical understanding itself is transferring."

Knowledge transfer. Through our joined hands, I could sense aspects of Rowan's magical training that should have taken years of study to understand. Ice magic wasn't just cold, it was architecture. And through our bond, I felt his growing awareness of sprite magic as something far more complex than simple light creation. My magic wasn't just bright, it was a blueprint.

"Continue the exercise," Professor Meridian instructed, though I could see from her expression that we'd already provided more data than she'd expected from a single collaborative casting.

The ward that emerged from our combined efforts was unlike anything I'd seen in three years of magical education. A barrier of crystalline light that looked like captured aurora, beautiful enough to serve as artwork but strong enough to stop a charging sleigh team. The magical density readings on Professor Meridian's instruments spiked into ranges that should have been impossible for student-level casting.

"Extraordinary," she breathed. "The magical integration is approaching permanent levels."

Permanent. The word echoed through our mental connection with implications that neither of us was ready to fully consider.

"Quite remarkable," Lady Silverleaf said, rising from her observation post with fluid grace. "Lord Darian will be most interested in today's developments."

The casual mention of Rowan's uncle made him tense beside me, his magical signature spiking with protective fury that immediately interfaced with mine in ways that sent visible aurora patterns dancing around our joined hands.

"Lady Silverleaf," Professor Meridian said with polite authority, "I trust your observations are purely academic in nature?"

"Of course," Lady Silverleaf replied with a smile that was all teeth and no warmth. "Though I believe the Winter Court's interest in Mr. Blackthorn's development predates his current...educational arrangement. Blood precedes charter."

The proprietary edge in her voice made it clear that as far as the Winter Court was concerned, Rowan belonged to them regardless of what academic choices he'd made or personal bonds he'd formed.

"Any such discussions would need to be arranged through proper academic channels," Professor Meridian said firmly. "North Pole University maintains strict protocols regarding external interference with student educational experiences."

"Miss Snowfall," Lady Silverleaf said as we prepared to leave, her voice carrying casual authority that made it clear this wasn't really a request. "Mr. Blackthorn. I wonder if you might have a few moments for an informal conversation?"

Through our bond, I felt Rowan's instant tension, along with his awareness that refusing would be perceived as uncooperative,, while agreeing would grant them exactly the kind of private access they wanted.

"Actually," Professor Meridian interjected smoothly, "I need both students to remain after class for debriefing on today's exercise. Academic protocol, you understand."

Lady Silverleaf's smile didn't waver, but something cold flickered behind her pale eyes. "Of course. Perhaps another time, when academic obligations permit."

As she glided from the classroom with predatory grace, Professor Meridian activated privacy wards that made the air shimmer with protective magic.

"You can't avoid them forever," she said quietly once the wards were in place. "The Winter Court has legal standing to request interviews with Mr. Blackthorn regardless of university preferences."

"What about Ivy?" Rowan asked, his voice tight with protective concern.

"Miss Snowfall's participation would be voluntary," Professor Meridian replied. "But refusing to cooperate while her partner is being questioned might be... strategically inadvisable."

"How long do we have?" I asked.

"Lord Darian has requested formal interviews for tomorrow afternoon," Professor Meridian admitted. "I've managed to ensure they'll be conducted on university grounds with faculty oversight. With oversight, we can halt the session when your runes hit a Level-3 flare. Without it, the Court's thresholds are... higher."

The implications hit like a cold weight in my chest. Tomorrow, we'd be questioned separately about our binding, our magical development, and our usefulness to their political objectives.

"What do we need to know?" I asked, because whatever was coming, we'd face it the same way we'd faced everything else since the binding began.

Together, even when they tried to separate us.

Especially then.

OUR SUITE's communication system chimed with an incoming message.

Mr. Blackthorn, Miss Snowfall: Formal interviews scheduled for tomorrow, 2:00 PM, Conference Room 7, Administrative Tower. Attendance required. Separate sessions for accuracy of information gathering. Duration approximately 90 minutes each. Academic Affairs.

Ninety minutes. As I reached for the message crystal to dismiss it, our hands brushed apart for just an instant, and both binding runes flared with urgent silver light. In the same moment, a faint aurora pattern flickered across the classroom windows, lasting just long enough for us to recognize the shape: three inter-locked snowflakes pulsing like a metronome.

Ninety minutes apart.

My throat went tight, then steady. The rune settled under Rowan's palm. The envoys could schedule whatever they liked; we would set the terms that mattered.

Together, I sent through our bond.

His answer landed warm as breath in cold air. *Always.*

CHAPTER TWELVE
DIVIDE & PRESSURE

ROWAN

The suite felt different when we returned from Professor Meridian's class.

Not physically, the same comfortable seating arrangements, the same warm lighting, the same magical amenities that had made sharing living space manageable rather than invasive. But something in the atmosphere had shifted, as if the Winter Court's growing interest had followed us home like a persistent shadow.

"They're going to try to separate us during the interviews," I said as we settled into our usual study positions. "Standard interrogation technique, divide the subjects, compare their stories, look for inconsistencies that can be exploited."

Through our bond, I felt Ivy's spike of anxiety at the prospect of facing Winter Court politics without the magical stability that physical contact provided. The proximity requirements had tightened to the point where even brief separations were becoming painful, and I suspected that was intentional rather than coincidental.

You think they're manipulating the binding somehow? she asked through our mental connection.

I think they're testing its limits to see how much control they can exert over our choices, I replied grimly. *Force us to choose between cooperation and comfort, then use our answers to shape their strategy.*

I moved from my chair to the couch where she was reviewing notes, settling beside her close enough that our thighs pressed together and our binding runes synchronized into their familiar rhythm. The relief was immediate and profound, not just the magical harmony, but the emotional steadiness that came from having her presence anchor my storm magic before it could turn destructive.

"We need protocols," Ivy said, her voice carrying the practical determination that had emerged over the past few days. "Fifteen minutes wrecked me yesterday; ninety looks like surgery without anesthetic."

She was right. We spent the next hour developing strategies that felt both necessary and slightly ridiculous, safe words to signal when either of us reached a magical threshold ("pine ward" for her, "winter solstice" for me), planned micro-breaks every eighteen minutes if the Court allowed them, breathing techniques to help stabilize each other's magic at a distance.

"Count three breaths," Ivy said, practicing the grounding sequence we'd developed. "Think of the pine ward scent from our first collaborative casting. Let my light magic hold the structure while your storm settles."

"If they cut sound wards, hum on the same pitch," I added, testing another technique. "If they force silence, visualize the same image. The aurora ward we made today, use the crystalline patterns as anchor points."

I watched her file away each instruction with the kind of methodical precision that surprised me. Just days ago, she'd been the sprite who tried to stay invisible. Now she was planning for a magical interrogation with strategic thinking that would have impressed court tacticians. When Ivy got scared, she got clinical, transforming fear into actionable intelligence, vulnerability into systematic preparation.

It should have felt like an academic exercise, preparing for what amounted to magical separation under hostile observation. Instead, it felt like partnership in the truest sense, two people who'd found each other planning how to survive being pulled apart.

"What are they likely to ask?" Ivy asked.

"Family history, magical development, political loyalties," I replied, automatically cataloguing the standard Winter Court interview protocol I'd been trained to expect since childhood. "But also personal questions designed to identify pressure points they can use later."

"Pressure points?"

"Things we care about enough to compromise for. People we'd protect regardless of cost. Fears that could be exploited to ensure compliance." I paused, realizing that the most dangerous pressure point was sitting right beside me. "They'll want to understand exactly what you mean to me, and what I'm willing to sacrifice to keep you safe."

Through our bond, I felt her sharp attention, along with her growing understanding that the interviews weren't just about gathering information. They were about mapping our emotional vulnerabilities so those vulnerabilities could be weaponized later.

"And what am I willing to sacrifice to keep you safe," she added quietly.

"Exactly."

THE ADMINISTRATIVE TOWER at two o'clock felt like walking into a trap disguised as bureaucracy.

Professor Blitzen met us at the entrance, her silver hair crackling with barely contained electrical energy and her expression carrying the kind of professional tension that suggested she'd spent the morning arguing with people who outranked her.

"Mr. Blackthorn," she said with formal courtesy that felt more protective than welcoming. "Miss Snowfall. The interviews will be conducted in Conference Rooms 7 and 9, with faculty oversight as previously agreed upon. Professor Meridian will observe Miss Snowfall's session, and I will monitor Mr. Blackthorn's."

Dylan appeared at her shoulder, his fox-shifter energy more subdued than usual. "I've set up monitoring equipment in both rooms," he said quietly. "If your binding runes hit Level-3 distress, we can halt the sessions immediately."

Level-3 distress. I'd never experienced magical separation severe enough to trigger the emergency protocols, but based on yesterday's fifteen-minute trial, ninety minutes felt like deliberate cruelty.

"Lord Darian and Lady Silverleaf are waiting," Professor Blitzen continued. "I want both of you to remember that this is still university territory, subject to academic rather than court jurisdiction. You have rights here that you wouldn't have in Winter Court proper."

Through our bond, I felt Ivy's mixture of determination and fear as she realized this was the last conversation we'd have before being deliberately separated for longer than we'd ever attempted.

"Remember the protocols," I said quietly, taking her hand one final time before the interviews began. "Remember that whatever they say, whatever they offer, whatever they threaten, we face it together even when we're apart."

"Together," she agreed, and the word carried the weight of a promise rather than a simple agreement.

Professor Blitzen gestured toward Conference Room 7. "Miss Snowfall, Professor Meridian is waiting for you. Mr. Blackthorn, Conference Room 9."

The moment our hands separated, my binding rune began its familiar warning pulse. Not painful yet, but insistent enough to remind me that every second of separation was being counted by magic that didn't care about Winter Court politics or academic protocols.

Conference Room 9 was smaller than I'd expected, with crystalline walls that probably facilitated magical monitoring and a table positioned to create intimacy rather than formal distance. Lord Darian was already seated, his pale eyes studying me with the kind of analytical intensity that had characterized our family interactions since my parents' deaths.

Lady Silverleaf occupied the chair beside him, her presence radiating the particular brand of predatory patience that marked Winter Court nobility at their most dangerous. Professor Blitzen took her position near the door, clearly prepared to intervene if the session moved beyond acceptable parameters.

"Nephew," Lord Darian said with the kind of false warmth that suggested this conversation would be anything but familial. "Thank you for making time in your academic schedule."

"Uncle," I replied with equal courtesy, settling into the chair across from them and trying to ignore the way my binding rune was already beginning to ache with Ivy's absence. "I understand the Winter Court has questions about my current... educational arrangements."

"Educational arrangements," Lady Silverleaf repeated with amusement that didn't reach her eyes. "Such a quaint way to describe magical binding with territorial implications."

The words hit exactly as intended, a reminder that whatever personal choices I thought I'd made, the Winter Court viewed them through the lens of political consequence rather than individual agency.

"Miss Snowfall seems like a charming young woman," Lord Darian continued with a casual observation that felt like calculation. "Bright, determined, surprisingly articulate for someone from such... modest magical heritage."

Modest magical heritage. The dismissive phrase was designed to remind me of the social gap between Winter Court nobility and whatever family background Ivy represented.

"Her magical heritage is complementary to mine," I replied carefully. "The binding wouldn't have been possible otherwise."

"Indeed," Lady Silverleaf murmured, consulting what appeared to be an official document with my family crest embossed at the top. "Which raises interesting questions about compatibility, choice, and the difference between magical coincidence and deliberate design."

Through our bond, I felt the first spike of real distress from Ivy's direction, not just separation anxiety, but something sharper that suggested her interview wasn't proceeding as diplomatically as mine.

"You seem distracted, nephew," Lord Darian observed. "Perhaps the binding is proving more...intrusive than you initially anticipated?"

The casual question felt like a probe for weakness, testing whether the forced separation was affecting my ability to focus on the political implications of their visit.

"I'm simply wondering why the Winter Court is so interested in an academic binding between two students," I replied, deflecting rather than acknowledging the growing pain that came from being magically separated from Ivy for longer than our bond could comfortably tolerate.

"Blood precedes charter," Lady Silverleaf said, echoing her earlier assertion with quiet authority. "You are Winter Court nobility, heir to one of our oldest bloodlines. Your magical development affects court interests regardless of where that development occurs."

"And Miss Snowfall's magical development?"

"Miss Snowfall," Lord Darian said with deliberate casualness, "appears to possess capabilities that weren't fully documented in her academic records. Capabilities that become quite remarkable when enhanced through partnership magic."

The observation felt like a trap. They knew something about Ivy's background that she didn't, and they were testing whether I knew it too.

"Partnership magic enhances compatible signatures," I replied neutrally. "That's well-established magical theory."

"To a point," Lady Silverleaf agreed. "But when enhancement approaches the level of fundamental magical transformation, theory becomes political reality."

Through our bond, I felt another spike of distress from Ivy, accompanied by what felt like magical resonance from unexpected sources. Not just our binding, but something else, like her magic was responding to information that was reshaping her understanding of her own capabilities.

My binding rune flared hot against my ribs, and I had to fight to keep my expression neutral as separation anxiety began to edge toward actual pain.

"You're in distress," Professor Blitzen observed from her position near the door. "We can take a break if needed."

"I'm fine," I said, though the lie was becoming harder to maintain as whatever was happening in Ivy's interview sent waves of confusion and alarm through our connection.

"The binding grows stronger each day," Lord Darian noted with clinical interest. "More dependent, more intrusive, more... permanent. That must be concerning for someone who values independence."

"I value partnership," I replied, letting some of my genuine conviction bleed through the diplomatic language. "I value collaboration over isolation."

"Even when that collaboration comes with political conse- quences you didn't choose?" Lady Silverleaf pressed. "Even when it affects your ability to fulfill family obligations that predate your current... educational interests?"

The words carried the weight of an ultimatum disguised as inquiry. They were offering me a choice: abandon the binding and return to Winter Court expectations, or face consequences that could extend far beyond academic inconvenience.

But before I could formulate a response that wouldn't commit me to anything irreversible, my binding rune spiked with such intensity that I actually gasped. The ache that had been building throughout the interview spread from my ribs into my chest, making each breath feel labored. My fingers began to tremble against the conference table, and I could see frost forming on my exhales, subtle signs of magical distress that I fought to keep controlled.

The effort of maintaining diplomatic composure while magical separation ate at my concentration was becoming impos- sible. Lord Darian's satisfied expression told me he could see exactly how much the enforced distance was costing me, and worse, he was enjoying it.

"Mr. Blackthorn," Professor Blitzen said sharply, moving toward the table as magical distress radiated from my binding rune with visible aurora patterns. "That's approaching Level-3. We need to halt this session."

"Just a few more minutes," Lord Darian said with the kind of authority that suggested he was accustomed to overruling academic protocols when they interfered with his objectives.

But Professor Blitzen's expression had shifted from protective to actively threatening, lightning dancing between her fingers with the promise of consequences that even Winter Court nobility couldn't ignore.

"The session is over," she declared with finality that made the room's temperature drop several degrees. "Mr. Blackthorn requires immediate medical attention."

As she moved to escort me from the conference room, I caught Lord Darian's satisfied expression, not disappointed that the interview had been cut short, but pleased that it had revealed exactly what he'd wanted to learn.

They hadn't been trying to gather information about our binding.

They'd been testing how much pain we could endure when separated, and how that pain could be used to control our choices.

The corridor outside Conference Room 9 felt like sanctuary and torture simultaneously, closer to Ivy, but still not close enough to end the desperate reaching sensation that was making my storm magic spike toward destructive chaos.

"Where is she?" I asked Professor Blitzen urgently.

"Conference Room 7. Professor Meridian ended her session at the same time." Professor Blitzen's voice carried grim satisfaction. "Whatever they thought they'd accomplish by pushing you both to magical breaking point, they've learned that university faculty won't be complicit in student endangerment."

But as we approached Conference Room 7, I could feel through our bond that whatever had happened during Ivy's interview had shaken her far more than simple separation anxiety. She'd learned something about herself, something that changed her understanding of who she was and why our binding had been so perfectly calibrated to our specific magical signatures.

The conference room door opened, and Ivy practically fell into my arms, her binding rune flaring so brightly it was visible through her sleeve. The moment our skin touched, the desperate magical reaching settled into harmony, but I could feel through our connection that the relief was temporary.

She gripped my sleeve too tight, her knuckles white with tension I'd never seen from her before. Her rune flickered like a storm lantern caught in the wind, the light pattern unstable in ways that spoke to fundamental shock rather than simple separation anxiety.

"What did they tell you?" I asked quietly, positioning myself to shield her from Professor Meridian's concerned observation. Whatever she'd learned, she needed time to process it without academic oversight.

"Things about my family," she whispered, her voice carrying tremors that had nothing to do with magical distress. "Things that don't make sense. Things that make our binding look less like a coincidence and more like..."

"More like what?"

"More like someone's been planning this for years."

Through the bond, I caught carefully controlled flashes of what she'd learned, fragments about her magical lineage that contradicted her parents' explanations, hints about capabilities that had been hidden rather than underdeveloped, suggestions that she'd been identified and monitored long before our binding had ever occurred. But underneath the specific revelations, I felt something deeper: the disorientation that came from discovering your entire understanding of yourself had been built on deliberate deception.

Professor Meridian appeared beside us, her wind sprite magic creating a privacy buffer that would prevent casual eavesdropping. "We need to get you both out of here," she said quietly. "The interviews revealed more than they should have, and there are people who won't be happy about how much you now know."

"Know about what?" I asked.

"About why your binding was so perfectly calibrated," she replied grimly. "And about who's been watching you both since long before you ever met."

As we made our way toward the Administrative Tower's exit, I felt Ivy's hand tighten around mine and her determination crystallizing into something that felt suspiciously like resolve.

Whatever secrets had been revealed during the interviews, whatever political games we'd been unknowingly playing, whatever forces had been shaping our lives from the shadows, we'd face them the same way we'd faced everything else since our binding began.

CHAPTER THIRTEEN
WHISPERS & WITNESSES

IVY

I pushed scrambled eggs around my plate, barely tasting them as Lady Silverleaf's words from three days ago replayed in my mind for the hundredth time.

"Your mother is descended from the Lux bloodline...court mages who served as architects for the original Winter Court magical infrastructure. Your father carries Niveus heritage...ice sprites whose family helped design the territorial magic that established NPU itself."

Lux and Niveus. Not the modest Arctic sprite lineage my parents had claimed. Families powerful enough that Winter Court had spent eighteen years tracking me, waiting for the right moment to activate a binding they'd designed specifically for my bloodline.

The letter I'd sent to my parents yesterday sat heavy in my thoughts. Short, direct questions that demanded real answers: "Who are we really? What else haven't you told me? Did you know this binding was coming?"

"...heard they can't be more than touching distance apart now..."

The whisper from a nearby table barely registered through my spiraling thoughts.

"...my roommate said they share dreams..."

I absently cut my toast into smaller and smaller pieces, reconstructing Lady Silverleaf's clinical assessment in my mind. "The binding you've experienced was not random. Your magical signatures were documented through The Concordance Index when you were both children, identified as compatible for territorial control applications."

"Ivy."

Rowan's mental voice cut through my obsessive review, gentle but insistent.

"You're broadcasting anxiety through the bond. And everyone's staring."

I looked up, suddenly aware that the Crystal Dining Hall had gone noticeably quieter around us. Students at nearby tables watched with the kind of fascinated speculation that turned people into entertainment rather than classmates. Some whispered behind hands, others openly documented us with assessment crystals that probably fed into research projects about partnership magic development.

"...Winter Court sent people to evaluate them personally..."

"...dangerous, that kind of binding..."

"It's like being a traveling exhibition," I muttered, setting down my fork as my appetite disappeared entirely.

Through our bond, I felt Rowan's understanding of what had been consuming my thoughts, along with his own complex feelings about the family secrets that were reshaping both our identities.

"The letter will reach them soon," he offered quietly through our mental connection. "And then we'll have real answers instead of just Winter Court propaganda."

"What if the real answers are worse?" I thought back.

Three days after the interviews, North Pole University had become a maze of hushed conversations that stopped whenever we appeared together. Not malicious, exactly, but intense...the kind of attention that made every public space feel like a performance we hadn't auditioned for.

"Ready?" Rowan asked aloud, extending his hand as we prepared to navigate the gauntlet of stares toward Advanced Theoretical Applications.

I took it, grateful for the steady warmth that anchored me when my own thoughts threatened to spiral into paranoia about bloodlines and breeding programs disguised as magical education.

Through our bond, I felt Rowan's grim amusement. *At least we're interesting. Better than invisible.*

Is it? I asked, noting how Marcus Thornfield's study group fell silent as we passed their usual table near the library entrance. *When was the last time anyone looked at us and saw students instead of a curiosity?*

The question hit deeper than I'd intended. I'd been invisible by choice for so long. Now visibility felt like being pinned under a magnifying glass, every gesture analyzed for meaning that might not exist.

"Miss Snowfall! Mr. Blackthorn!"

The voice that called our names belonged to Frost Silverleaf, and the cheerful tone made my stomach clench with warning. She approached with two other senior winter magic students, Gareth Coldmere, whose pale eyes held calculating intelligence, and a girl I recognized but had never spoken to, both wearing expressions of friendly interest that felt as genuine as decorative ice.

"How are you both adjusting to all the attention?" Frost asked with the kind of casual concern that suggested genuine sympathy. "It must be overwhelming, having your private magical development become such a public fascination."

"We're managing," Rowan replied carefully, his voice carrying polite distance that didn't quite mask his wariness.

"Of course you are," Gareth said, his tone carrying subtle weight. "Though some students are wondering whether the attention is entirely fair. Special accommodations, modified schedules, and faculty oversight that other students don't receive. Whether magical binding should grant preferential treatment."

The words were carefully chosen, not accusatory, but inviting us to acknowledge that our situation created inequities that affected other students' educational experiences.

"We didn't request special treatment," I said, feeling heat creep up my neck. "The accommodations were necessary to prevent magical chaos that could have endangered everyone."

"Naturally," Frost agreed with delicate hesitation. "Though you have to admit, your magical development has been quite remarkable since the binding began. Some students wonder whether partnership magic might offer enhancements that individual study can't match."

Through our bond, I felt Rowan's sharp attention as he recognized the trap being laid. This wasn't a concern, it was testing our response to pressure disguised as peer sympathy.

"Partnership magic requires compatible signatures and mutual consent," Rowan said firmly. "It can't be artificially induced for academic benefit."

"Mutual consent," Gareth repeated thoughtfully. "Interesting phrase, given that your binding began with a cursed charm rather than a deliberate choice. There's a difference, isn't there, between genuine choice and practical accommodation?"

The question struck exactly where he'd intended it to. How much of our partnership was choice, and how much was magical compulsion?

Before either of us could respond, a new voice cut through the tension with familiar authority.

"Miss Silverleaf," Professor Meridian said, appearing beside our group with perfectly timed intervention. "I believe you have a ward construction exercise scheduled for this period?"

"Yes, Professor," Frost replied with immediate compliance. "We were just discussing partnership magic theory."

"Perhaps you could discuss it during your own collaborative exercises rather than interrogating other students," Professor Meridian said with dry observation. The dismissal was polite, professional, and absolutely clear. Frost and her companions took the hint with graceful retreat that didn't quite mask their satisfaction at having planted seeds of doubt about our situation.

"Interesting perspective on choice and necessity," Frost said as they prepared to leave. "Something to think about, certainly."

As they walked away, I felt the weight of their conversation settling like cold stone in my chest. Not because their questions were wrong, but because they touched fears I'd been trying not to acknowledge.

"How much of this is real?" I asked Rowan quietly as we continued toward our classroom. "How much of what we feel for each other is genuine, and how much is magical compulsion?"

Through our bond, I felt his understanding of the question, along with his own complicated relationship with the same doubts.

"I don't know," he admitted honestly. "But I know that questioning it doesn't change how it feels."

How it feels. The phrase carried weight that went beyond magical compatibility or practical accommodation. Whatever forces had brought us together, whatever compulsions shaped our daily choices, the emotional reality of our partnership felt genuine in ways that had nothing to do with binding runes or proximity requirements.

"Professor Meridian," I said as we reached the classroom entrance, "can I ask you something about partnership magic theory?"

"Certainly," she replied, though her pale green eyes held the wariness of someone who suspected the question would be more personal than academic.

"Is it possible to distinguish between magical attraction and genuine emotional connection when the two are intertwined from the beginning?"

Professor Meridian studied us both for a moment, her wind sprite instincts clearly reading emotional undercurrents that we might not be fully aware of ourselves.

"Miss Snowfall," she said finally, "in my experience, genuine emotional connection doesn't require magical enhancement to be profound. But magical compatibility can reveal emotional truths that might otherwise remain hidden."

"Meaning?"

"Meaning," she continued with gentle authority, "that if your feelings for each other were purely magical compulsion, the binding wouldn't be stabilizing the way it has. Forced connections create resistance, not harmony."

The observation should have been reassuring. Instead, it reminded me how much our lives had become subject to analysis by people who studied our relationship like an academic exercise rather than a lived experience.

But as we entered the classroom and took our usual positions at the demonstration table, I felt something settle in my chest that had nothing to do with magical theory and everything to do with the simple reality of having Rowan beside me.

Whatever questions other people raised about choice and necessity, whatever doubts they planted about the authenticity of our connection, the emotional truth remained constant: being with him felt like home in ways that had nothing to do with binding runes or academic accommodation.

And if that was magical compulsion, it was the kind of compulsion I could choose to accept.

THE DREAM CAME that night with the clarity of shared experience rather than individual sleep.

I was standing in a place I'd never seen but somehow recognized, a crystalline chamber beneath North Pole University, carved from ice that held aurora patterns within its depths. Ancient runes covered the walls, pulsing with soft light that responded to magical presence.

But I wasn't alone.

Rowan stood beside me, his dark hair catching the aurora glow and his pale eyes reflecting depths that seemed to hold centuries of winter magic. Through the dream-bond, I could feel his thoughts merging with mine in ways that went far beyond our waking connection.

This place, his dream-voice carried certainty that felt like recognition. *It's real. Somewhere beneath the campus.*

How do you know? I asked, though the chamber felt familiar to me too, like a place I'd seen in half-remembered stories.

Because this is where it all began, he replied, gesturing toward the runes that decorated the crystalline walls. *The first Winter*

Court binding. The original partnership magic that created the territorial foundation for everything that followed.

As he spoke, the runes began to glow brighter, and I realized they weren't just decorative, they were instructional. Showing us techniques, principles, applications of partnership magic that exceeded anything in current academic literature.

Someone wanted us to find this, I realized with growing certainty. *The shared dream, the specific location, the teaching runes, this isn't accidental.*

No, Rowan agreed grimly. *But the question is whether we're being guided by someone who wants to help us, or someone who wants to control us.*

Through the dream-connection, I caught flashes of his deeper fears, that our binding had been engineered not just to create partnership, but to give others leverage over our choices. That the shared dream was another form of manipulation disguised as revelation.

But as we moved deeper into the crystalline chamber, studying runes that seemed to respond to our combined magical signatures, I felt something else. Not manipulation, but invitation. The chamber wanted us here, wanted us to understand what we were becoming.

Look, I said, pointing toward a section of wall where the runes formed patterns that looked almost like... *Portrait galleries.*

The carved sections showed partnerships throughout history, two figures whose magic intertwined in displays of collaborative power that exceeded individual capabilities. Not just magical enhancement, but transformation. People who had become something new through choosing each other.

They're all different, Rowan observed, studying the portraits with academic fascination. *Different magical types, different time* periods, *different applications. However, the underlying principle remains consistent, partnership as an evolutionary process rather than mere cooperation.*

And they all chose, I added, noting the way each portrait showed deliberate gesture, hands extended in offers that had been accepted rather than compelled. *Whatever brought them together initially, they chose to become what they became.*

The observation settled something in my chest that had been aching since Frost Silverleaf's conversation. These partnerships hadn't been diminished by questions of choice versus necessity, they had been defined by the choice to embrace what they could become together.

As the dream began to fade with approaching dawn, I felt one final insight crystallize with the certainty of truth rather than hope:

Whatever had initiated our binding, whatever forces continued to shape our development, the choice of what to become with it remained ours.

And I knew, with clarity that exceeded anything I'd ever felt while awake, that I would choose Rowan again. Not because magic compelled me, but because the person I became when I was with him was someone I wanted to continue being.

Even if it meant facing whatever consequences that choice would bring.

Together, I whispered as the crystalline chamber dissolved into ordinary sleep.

Always, came his reply, warm as breath against winter air.

When I woke, the binding rune on my wrist was glowing softly with residual dream-magic, and through our connection, I could feel Rowan stirring in his own bed with the same sense of revelation and resolve.

The chamber was real. The choice was ours.

And whatever forces wanted to use those facts against us would discover that some partnerships were stronger than the people who tried to control them.

CHAPTER FOURTEEN

THE TEST OF LOYALTY

ROWAN

The summons came at dawn, delivered with the kind of formal courtesy that made refusal impossible while maintaining the illusion of choice.

Mr. Blackthorn, Miss Snowfall: Your presence is required for a collaborative demonstration at 1:00 PM, Observatory Main Lecture Hall. This presentation will showcase partnership magic development for visiting academic observers. Attendance required for observers; encouraged for subjects. , Academic Affairs

Through our bond, I felt Ivy's spike of anxiety as she read the message, along with her growing understanding that we were being maneuvered into another performance for people whose interests didn't align with our own.

"They're not requesting," I said quietly. "They're commanding, politely."

The Winter Court envoys? Ivy asked through our mental connection.

Almost certainly. This feels like the next phase of whatever strategy they've been developing since the interviews.

We'd been anticipating something like this for the past two days, ever since Professor Meridian had mentioned increased "interest" from external magical authorities in our partnership development. The kind of interest that came with official observation, formal evaluation, and political consequences that could range from inconvenient to catastrophic.

"What do you think they want to see?" Ivy asked aloud as we made our way toward breakfast, our joined hands drawing the usual mixture of curious glances and speculative whispers from other students.

"Evidence," I replied grimly. "Either that we're too dangerous to continue without intervention, or that we're useful enough to be worth controlling."

Through our bond, I felt her understanding of the trap we were walking into. Public demonstration meant witnesses, documentation, and magical readings that could be analyzed for vulnerabilities or exploited for political advantage. Whatever we chose to show, and whatever we tried to hide, would become part of a formal record that could be used against us later.

The Observatory Main Lecture Hall had been transformed into something that resembled a court proceeding more than an academic presentation. Tiered seating faced a central demonstration platform, with monitoring equipment positioned to capture every aspect of magical output. But it was the back section that made my stomach clench with political recognition.

Lord Darian sat with Lady Silverleaf and two other Winter Court representatives, their pale eyes studying the setup with analytical intensity. They weren't here to observe academic progress, they were here to set parameters under pressure.

"Mr. Blackthorn, Miss Snowfall," Professor Blitzen announced as we entered, her voice carrying official neutrality that didn't quite mask her protective concern. "Thank you for participating in today's demonstration of partnership magic development."

The formal introduction felt like a warning disguised as courtesy. We were being presented as willing participants in what amounted to political theater, with our cooperation serving someone else's agenda regardless of our personal preferences.

Dylan and Lyra were positioned near the monitoring equipment, their expressions carefully professional. As we moved into position, Lyra caught my eye and whispered quietly, "If the crest appears, it's not you losing control, it's the binding asserting design."

The demonstration targets were more complex than anything we'd worked with in normal classes, crystalline constructs that shifted position, changed magical signatures, and generated interference patterns designed to test adaptive collaboration under stress.

"Begin when ready," Professor Blitzen announced.

I looked at Ivy, noting the determined set of her shoulders and the way her light magic was already responding to the proximity of my frost power. Through our bond, I felt her resolve to give them a performance worth watching, regardless of the political consequences.

Together? I asked through our mental connection.

Together, she confirmed.

We reached for our magic simultaneously, letting the binding's enhanced synchronization guide our collaborative casting. The ward that began to form between us was immediately more complex than anything we'd created in controlled classroom settings, layers of crystalline light reinforced with frost patterns.

Then our ward pinched into angles we hadn't chosen. Three

snowflakes locked into a triangle, clean, heraldic, inevitable. The Winter Court staring back at us from our own hands.

The binding rune flared against my ribs, hot and insistent, sending needles of ice-burn through my chest. Beside me, Ivy swayed slightly, her knees dipping as the magical hijack sent waves of nausea through our connection. I steadied her with my free hand, our physical contact helping to anchor us both against the coercion.

"Fascinating," Lady Silverleaf murmured from her observation position, her voice carrying satisfaction that made my blood run cold. "Hereditary recognition is... reassuring."

Hereditary recognition. The phrase meant our magic was responding to bloodline influences that predated our conscious choices, Winter Court magical signatures that had been embedded in the binding itself, designed to surface during demonstrations exactly like this one.

I tried to modify the ward's formation, to redirect our combined magic away from the emerging crest pattern. But resistance fed the pattern. That was the cruelty of it.

If they want a demonstration, Ivy sent, steel under starlight, *we'll give them ours.*

She fed the crest, then rewrote it. Frost lines curved into aurora filigree; light braided through winter geometry until their emblem became ours. Through our bond, I felt her invitation for me to join her choice.

I let my frost magic flow into her modified design, adding structural elements that turned the Winter Court crest into something that belonged to us rather than them. The result was breathtaking, a ward that looked like captured starlight, strong enough to stop a charging sleigh team but beautiful enough to hang in a museum.

The lecture hall had gone completely silent.

Professor Blitzen breathed, a visible arc of lightning fingering the monitors as she said, "That's enough." Her academic excitement overrode whatever political concerns she might have had. "The magical density and artistic integration are unlike anything in current partnership magic literature."

Through our bond, I felt Ivy's mixture of satisfaction and exhaustion as our collaborative casting settled into harmony. We'd been maneuvered into revealing capabilities we'd preferred to keep private, but we'd done so on our own terms rather than as unwilling subjects of Winter Court manipulation.

"Quite remarkable," Lord Darian said, rising from his observation position with the kind of satisfied authority that suggested the demonstration had served his purposes perfectly. "The hereditary recognition patterns are even stronger than initial reports indicated."

"Hereditary patterns we modified according to our own artistic vision," Ivy said with quiet firmness that carried across the entire lecture hall. "Whatever influences shaped the foundation, the final result represents our conscious choices."

"Indeed," Lady Silverleaf agreed with a smile that was all teeth and no warmth. "Though one wonders whether conscious choice remains relevant when hereditary magic is so... insistent about proper expression."

The words hung in the air like a threat disguised as observation. Through our bond, I felt Ivy's understanding that we'd just been warned about the limits of our agency, that whatever choices we thought we were making, Winter Court legacy would ultimately determine the results.

"The demonstration is concluded," Professor Blitzen announced with the kind of protective authority that suggested she was prepared to end this political theater before it could escalate further. "Thank you all for your attendance."

As the observers began filing out, many stealing glances at the aurora patterns still dancing across the lecture hall's ceiling, I caught Dylan's expression of concerned calculation. Whatever had happened during our demonstration, it had revealed more about our binding's nature than any of us had expected.

"Mr. Blackthorn," Lord Darian said as he prepared to leave, his voice carrying casual authority that suggested private conversation rather than public address. "Perhaps we might continue our discussion from the other day? I believe recent developments have created new opportunities for mutual understanding."

"Modifiable is more reassuring," I replied diplomatically.

Through our bond, I felt Ivy's spike of alarm at the implications of his words. Not just another attempt to separate us, but something more direct, political pressure designed to force choices that would serve Winter Court interests regardless of our personal preferences.

As the Winter Court representatives departed with expressions of polite satisfaction, Dylan and Lyra exchanged a look that carried the weight of new discoveries. Whatever they'd seen in the monitoring data, it was significant enough to warrant private discussion.

"There will be a faculty vote tonight," Professor Blitzen said quietly as the lecture hall emptied around us. "Whether outside supervision is mandated for partnership magic development." Her expression was grim. "The demonstration gave them exactly the evidence they needed."

Through the Observatory's crystalline windows, I could see NPU's protective wards flickering in patterns that matched the crest geometry we'd just created, aurora traces synchronizing with the campus lattice in ways that suggested our legacy signature had just integrated deeper with the university's magical infrastructure.

"What do we do now?" Ivy asked quietly.

"We prepare for whatever they're planning next," I replied, though I could feel through our bond that both of us understood the situation was rapidly moving beyond our ability to control.

The demonstration had been a test of loyalty disguised as academic presentation. And judging by the satisfied expressions on Winter Court faces, we'd revealed exactly what they'd hoped to see.

CHAPTER FIFTEEN

BREAKING POINT

IVY

The faculty vote was scheduled for eight o'clock that evening in the Administrative Tower's council chambers, a formal session that would determine whether "external supervision" became mandatory for all partnership magic development at North Pole University.

Which meant, in practical terms, whether Rowan and I would be handed over to Winter Court control disguised as academic oversight.

"They're calling it a safety measure," Dylan said grimly as he briefed us in the Observatory's main lab. "Professor Ember has been pushing for it since yesterday's demonstration, claiming that unsupervised partnership magic poses unacceptable risks to campus stability."

He gestured toward the monitoring displays, where yesterday's readings still showed elevated baselines. "Your spectral integration is still elevated from the demonstration. The magical load hasn't fully normalized."

Through our bond, I felt Rowan's sharp spike of anger at the mention of Professor Ember's name. We'd both noticed her during the demonstration, taking notes with clinical intensity, watching us with something that felt more like calculation than curiosity.

"Professor Ember wasn't even present for most of our training sessions," I said, trying to keep my voice level despite the growing anxiety that had been building since we'd learned about the vote. "How can she assess the risks of our magical development?"

"She can't," Lyra replied with the kind of frustrated authority that came from too many encounters with academic politics. "But she doesn't need to. The Winter Court's formal interest in your partnership gives weight to any safety concerns she raises, regardless of their factual basis."

Safety concerns. The euphemism made my light magic flicker with indignation I struggled to control. Yesterday's demonstration had been successful by every objective measure, complex ward construction, collaborative magical integration, adaptive response to coercive influences. If anything, we'd proven that partnership magic could be both powerful and precisely controlled.

But precision and control weren't the point. The point was establishing precedent for Winter Court intervention in academic affairs, using our binding as justification for broader authority over magical education.

"What's the likely outcome?" Rowan asked with careful neutrality.

"Split vote," Dylan admitted. "Meridian, Blitzen, and most of the theoretical magic faculty support academic independence. Ember and the practical applications departments favor external oversight. If the motion passes, oversight is immediate and retroactive."

"And if we're supervised, they can legally compel demonstrations," Rowan added grimly.

Through our bond, I felt his understanding of what that meant. Administrators who would sacrifice our autonomy to avoid conflict with Winter Court authority, regardless of long-term implications.

"We could petition the vote," Lyra suggested without much conviction. "Request additional time to demonstrate that our partnership doesn't require external supervision."

"On what grounds?" Rowan asked. "That we've successfully integrated magical signatures that were designed to be controlled by Winter Court influences? That we've learned to work with hereditary patterns rather than resist them?"

The bitterness in his voice carried the weight of someone who'd grown up understanding that individual preference mattered less than political convenience when Winter Court interests were involved.

"On the grounds that we're students who deserve the same educational opportunities as everyone else," I said, surprising myself with the firmness in my voice. "That our magical development shouldn't be subject to external authority just because it's inconvenient for people who profit from keeping partnership magic suppressed."

Through our bond, I felt Rowan's sharp attention, along with his growing realization that I wasn't going to accept political maneuvering as inevitable. Three weeks ago, I might have. Three weeks ago, I would have found reasons to acquiesce rather than fight against institutional pressure.

But three weeks ago, I hadn't discovered what it felt like to have a partner worth defending.

"The vote is in two hours," Dylan said quietly. "Whatever we're going to do, we need to decide quickly."

Before anyone could respond, the Observatory's communication system chimed with an incoming message that made my binding rune pulse with warning.

Miss Snowfall: Your presence is requested in Conference Room 12 at 7:30 PM for preliminary discussion regarding partnership magic oversight protocols. This meeting precedes tonight's faculty vote. , Academic Affairs

Preliminary discussion. Another euphemism for individual pressure designed to soften resistance before the formal decision.

"They're separating us again," I said, noting that the message was addressed to me alone rather than both of us. "Trying to influence my position before the vote."

"Don't go," Rowan said immediately, his protective instincts flaring through our connection. "Whatever they want to discuss, it can include both of us or neither of us."

But even as he spoke, I could feel the political trap closing around us. Refusing to attend would be seen as uncooperative, while attending would give them exactly the kind of individual access they needed to apply pressure that would be harder to resist without our bond's stabilizing influence.

"I'll go," I decided, feeling his immediate opposition through our connection. "But only if they agree to limit the separation to thirty minutes. Any longer and the bond stress will undermine whatever they're trying to accomplish anyway."

Through our bond, I felt his mixture of pride and fear, pride that I was choosing to face the pressure directly, fear that I was underestimating the forces that would be brought to bear against our partnership.

Be careful, he said through our mental connection. *They'll offer things that sound reasonable but serve their interests rather than ours.*

I know, I replied, though part of me wondered whether

knowing would be enough when facing Winter Court political expertise.

CONFERENCE ROOM 12 was smaller and more intimate than previous spaces, soft lighting, comfortable seating, designed to encourage honest conversation. The crystal fixtures hummed with a tri-pulse cadence that felt oddly familiar.

Professor Ember was waiting, her expression carrying maternal concern that felt professionally calculated.

"Miss Snowfall," she said with welcoming warmth. "Thank you for taking the time to discuss these important matters."

"Professor," I replied carefully, settling across from her while monitoring the binding rune's response to separation from Rowan. Uncomfortable but manageable.

"No one questions your abilities or genuine care for Mr. Blackthorn," Professor Ember continued with diplomatic precision. "Your magical development has been remarkable."

She leaned forward slightly. "However, remarkable development comes with responsibilities students aren't prepared to handle alone. The Winter Court's offer isn't punishment, it's protection from forces that see partnership magic as either a threat to eliminate or a resource to exploit."

"Protection from what?" I asked.

"From magical politics that have been developing for centuries," she replied with apparent concern. "Miss Snowfall, you're talented but inexperienced, suddenly at the center of forces beyond your understanding. The Winter Court can provide guidance, and I can offer something concrete."

Her voice carried new authority. "Temporary amnesty for Mr. Blackthorn's prior incidents. A bespoke proximity exemption for classes, fewer disruptions. All contingent on accepting supervision."

The offer was reasonable, tempting, and utterly patronizing. Through our bond, I felt Rowan's distant presence anchoring me to who I was when I wasn't being managed.

"And if we prefer to develop our partnership without external guidance?" I asked.

"Then you'll face pressures that could destroy not just your academic future, but your personal safety," Professor Ember said gravely. "There are factions who view unsupervised partnership magic as an existential threat. People who would prefer elimination to control."

Through our bond, I felt the first spike of real separation anxiety as our conversation extended beyond twenty minutes. A high-pitched ice-chime rang in my ears, the same sound from yesterday's demonstration when the crest had formed without our consent. "But your input could influence tonight's outcome. A statement supporting oversight protocols would carry significant weight."

"And if I don't?"

"Then you'll face consequences much less pleasant than cooperative supervision."

The threat was subtle but clear. But as the binding rune flared with separation stress and I felt Rowan's growing concern, something crystallized in my chest, personal choice over political convenience.

"Professor Ember," I said quietly, rising with calm determination, "supervision that costs me my choice isn't protection."

Her expression shifted from maternal concern to something sharper. "You're eighteen with no experience in magical politics. You don't understand what you're refusing."

"I understand that I'm being asked to trade my autonomy for

someone else's definition of safety," I replied, moving toward the door as the binding rune's insistence became impossible to ignore. "And that's not a trade I'm willing to make."

"The Winter Court doesn't take refusal well," she called after me. "If you won't accept supervision willingly, they'll find other ways."

I paused at the threshold. "Then they'll discover that some partnerships are harder to control than they anticipated."

The corridor outside Conference Room 12 felt like freedom after political suffocation. But as I made my way back toward the Observatory, the binding rune's separation anxiety intensified to the point where each step felt like swimming against an increasingly strong current.

By the time I reached the main lab, I was dizzy with magical distress that had nothing to do with political pressure and everything to do with being apart from Rowan for longer than our bond could comfortably tolerate.

He was waiting at the Observatory's entrance, his face pale with the same separation anxiety I was experiencing. The moment our hands touched, the desperate reaching sensation settled into harmony, but I could feel through our connection that thirty minutes had pushed both of us closer to the edge of what was magically sustainable.

"How did it go?" Dylan asked, noting our obvious distress with professional concern.

"Professor Ember wanted me to publicly endorse Winter Court supervision," I said, settling beside Rowan close enough that our binding runes synchronized into their familiar rhythm. "I declined."

Through our bond, I felt his mixture of pride and alarm, pride that I'd refused to be manipulated, alarm at what my refusal would mean for the evening's vote.

"She also mentioned that there are factions who view unsupervised partnership magic as an existential threat," I added, wanting everyone to understand the stakes we were facing. "People who would prefer elimination to control."

"Elimination," Lyra repeated with the kind of academic precision that turned threats into research problems. "That's escalation beyond political maneuvering."

"Which means tonight's vote isn't just about supervision," Rowan said grimly. "It's about whether NPU can protect students from Winter Court authority, or whether we become the first casualties of a political conflict that's bigger than our individual partnership."

Before anyone could respond, the Observatory's main displays flickered with emergency announcements that made my stomach clench with dread.

Emergency Faculty Meeting relocated to the Main Auditorium due to unexpected attendance. Vote on Partnership Magic Oversight Protocols scheduled for 8:00 PM. Public observation permitted.

Public observation permitted.

The faculty vote had become a campus-wide spectacle, which meant that whatever happened tonight would be witnessed by hundreds of students whose opinions would shape the future of partnership magic at NPU.

Before we could leave for the Main Auditorium, the Observatory's main entrance chimed. Petal Brightwood entered with Marcus Thornfield and, surprisingly, Frost Silverleaf. The trio represented a cross-section of campus opinion that made my stomach clench with political awareness.

"We heard about the vote," Petal said without preamble, her flower magic creating subtle warmth in the air around us. "We'll stand with you. If they punish you, they punish all of us."

Marcus nodded with grudging respect. "Precision like yours doesn't need a leash."

But Frost's smile was sharp as winter glass. "Or maybe it does," she said sweetly. "Some partnerships require... guidance."

Through our bond, I felt Rowan's mixture of gratitude and wariness. Support from unexpected quarters, opposition from predictable ones, and the growing awareness that our partnership had become a symbol for larger questions about student autonomy and institutional control.

"Are you ready for this?" he asked quietly.

I looked around the Observatory's main lab, at Dylan and Lyra's protective concern, at the monitoring equipment that had documented our magical development, at the space where we'd discovered what partnership could become when it was chosen rather than imposed.

"I'm ready to fight for what we've built," I said, and meant it completely.

The binding rune pulsed with warm light that had nothing to do with Winter Court influence and everything to do with the choice to defend something worth preserving.

Whatever came next, we'd face it the way we'd faced everything else since our binding began.

Together, even when they tried to pull us apart.

Especially then.

But as we prepared to leave for the Main Auditorium, a wave of exhaustion hit me with such force that I stumbled against Rowan's shoulder. Not separation anxiety this time, something deeper, like the magical strain was finally catching up.

"Ivy?" Rowan's voice carried sharp concern as he steadied me. "What's wrong?"

"I don't know," I admitted, fighting dizziness that seemed to come from the binding itself. I tried the breathing protocol we'd developed, three breaths, pine ward scent, let his winter magic anchor mine. It failed completely.

The binding rune flared with sudden, overwhelming heat. Through our connection, I felt Rowan's alarm spike as the magical backlash from yesterday's forced demonstration finally hit us both.

My knees buckled. The last thing I saw was the tri-pulse cadence from Conference Room 12 flickering across the Observatory's crystal walls, three interlocked snowflakes pulsing like an accepted invitation.

"Level-4, integrity breach!" Dylan shouted.

The lights cut.

CHAPTER SIXTEEN
SECRETS REVEALED

ROWAN

The Observatory's medical bay had been designed for minor magical mishaps, overextended casting, potion accidents, the occasional aurora burn from students who got too close to active displays. It wasn't equipped for Level-4 binding integrity failures, but it was the closest private space where Dylan and Lyra could monitor Ivy's condition without campus-wide spectacle.

I sat beside her bed, maintaining skin contact through her limp hand while our binding runes pulsed in slow, unsteady rhythm. Three hours since she'd collapsed, and her magical signature still felt fragmented, like something fundamental had been torn rather than simply strained.

"Any change?" Professor Meridian asked, entering with the quiet authority that had made her our most reliable faculty ally. Her wind sprite magic created gentle air currents that carried the scent of pine and winter snow, comforting rather than clinical.

"Stable but distant," I replied, not taking my eyes off Ivy's pale face. "Whatever caused the backlash, it's not resolving naturally."

Through our bond, I could feel her consciousness like an echo, present but unreachable, as if she was trapped somewhere between sleeping and waking. Not quite comatose, but too far away for our mental connection to bridge the gap effectively.

"The faculty vote concluded an hour ago," Professor Meridian said quietly. "I thought you should know the outcome before you hear it through official channels."

I looked up sharply, noting the careful neutrality in her expression that suggested the news wouldn't be welcome. "External supervision?"

"Approved, seven votes to five. Professor Ember's faction prevailed, with administrative support citing safety concerns raised by Miss Snowfall's collapse." Professor Meridian's voice carried frustration that professional courtesy couldn't quite disguise. "Oversight begins immediately for all partnership magic activities."

Oversight begins immediately. Which meant that the moment Ivy woke up, we'd be subject to Winter Court supervision that would effectively end our autonomy while legitimizing political control through academic channels.

"They used her collapse as evidence?" I asked, fury building in my chest like the storm magic I'd learned to suppress.

"Professor Ember argued that Level-4 binding failures demonstrate the inherent instability of unsupervised partnership magic," Professor Meridian replied grimly. "The vote was cast as an emergency safety measure to prevent future incidents."

Perfect. Ivy had collapsed from magical strain caused by Winter Court manipulation, and they were using that collapse to justify the very oversight that had caused the problem in the first place. Political efficiency disguised as protective concern.

"There's something else," Professor Meridian continued, reaching into her robes to withdraw a crystalline message tube.

Unlike Winter Court correspondence's sharp edges and electric chill, this one pulsed with soft aurora light and emanated warmth like hearth-fire. "This arrived for Miss Snowfall during the vote. Given her current condition, I thought you might need to review its contents."

The message tube carried magical signatures I didn't recognize, older and more complex than Court magic. I broke the seal carefully, bracing for ward defenses that would trigger if I wasn't authorized. Nothing. Just warmth, trust, and the scent of pine forests in winter.

The message crystal emerged glowing with architectural illumination that reminded me of Ivy's magical signature, but deeper and more sophisticated.

Dearest Ivy, the crystalline script began, *we hope this reaches you safely and in time. The awakening of your binding marks the end of the protection that has kept you hidden for eighteen years.*

My stomach dropped. Hidden. Not overlooked, deliberately concealed from people who'd been hunting her.

We are not the Arctic sprites we claimed to be.

The second pulse of information flooded through the crystal, carrying genealogical details that made my understanding of everything snap into place. The aurora wards we'd seen, the way her magic interfaced so perfectly with architectural magic, the reason our binding had shown such sophisticated integration patterns.

Your mother is descended from the Lux bloodline, court mages who served as architects for the original Winter Court magical infrastructure. Your father carries Niveus heritage, ice sprites whose family helped design the territorial magic that established NPU itself.

She wasn't just any sprite. She was descended from the families who'd built the magical foundations that Winter Court authority rested on.

The third pulse carried the most damaging revelation, and with it came fury that built in my chest like storm magic. Frost condensed on the medical bay's rail, then cracked as my magic spiked beyond careful control. Only Ivy's pulse through our bond pulled me back from letting the storm loose entirely.

The binding you've experienced was not random. Your magical signatures were documented through The Concordance Index when you were both children, identified as compatible for territorial control applications. The charm that initiated your connection was placed deliberately, designed to surface when your development reached sufficient sophistication.

The Concordance Index. A breeding program disguised as academic research, identifying children whose combined magic could serve Winter Court territorial ambitions.

The knowledge we've enclosed will help you understand both what you're capable of and what forces will try to control that capability. The message continued with information that transformed understanding into power. *The runes we're sharing match those of the Founding Chamber, the chamber that your architectural heritage gives you the right to access.*

The dream chamber. The crystalline space beneath NPU that had felt so familiar because her bloodline had helped design it.

Remember, your light was never meant to be small. Only structural.

The message dissolved, leaving behind only the warm glow of family magic and the crystalline repository of knowledge that would fundamentally change Ivy's understanding of her own capabilities.

"Her parents have been hiding her from Winter Court attention for eighteen years," I said quietly, the magnitude of the deception finally settling in. "They're not arctic sprites, they're descended from the families who built the magical infrastructure that NPU and the Winter Court still use today."

Professor Meridian's expression grew troubled. "Which explains why your binding showed such sophisticated integration patterns. You weren't just compatible by accident, you were selected specifically because your magical signatures would create territorial magic capable of challenging Winter Court authority."

"Or serving it, if they could control us," I added grimly.

"Indeed. The question now is whether Miss Snowfall will choose to use that heritage to fight the oversight mandate, or whether the knowledge will make her a target too valuable for the Winter Court to release."

Through our bond, I felt Ivy's consciousness growing stronger, responding to the influx of ancestral knowledge like a plant reaching toward sunlight. The message dissolved, leaving behind only warm light and a crystalline knowledge repository.

Her eyes opened.

"The hallway wards are misaligned by two degrees," she said immediately, her voice hoarse but certain. "I can feel the drag against the building's foundation lattice."

I stared at her. Three hours ago, she'd been unconscious from magical backlash. Now she was diagnosing architectural problems in infrastructure she'd never studied.

"The message from your parents," I said gently, helping her sit up while maintaining contact. "They explained about your heritage, about The Concordance Index."

"Not hidden," she said with growing certainty that carried the weight of inherited memory. "Protected. Until I was strong enough to choose for myself."

Through our bond, I felt her awareness expanding as the architectural magic knowledge integrated with her existing abilities. Not just enhancement, but transformation, she was becoming someone who could work with magical infrastructure at levels that exceeded current academic theory.

"The faculty vote?" she asked.

"Supervision approved. We're officially under Winter Court oversight as of tonight."

Her expression hardened with resolve that belonged to someone who'd just discovered they carried the magical legacy of two families who'd helped shape the world the Winter Court now tried to control.

"No," she said quietly. "We're not."

"Ivy..."

"My parents spent eighteen years keeping me hidden so I could choose when I was ready," she continued. "I'm ready. And I choose to fight."

She lifted her free hand, fingers sketching patterns in the air above our joined palms. The medical bay's containment lattice dropped a pitch as her new geometry slipped into place, ambient hum stabilizing, monitors reading cleaner than they had all evening.

Dylan's eyebrows shot up from his monitoring station. "That shouldn't be possible without access codes."

"I don't need access codes," Ivy said simply. "My family built the foundation protocols."

Through our bond, I felt the truth of her words resonating with magic that drew from centuries of court architectural knowledge. She wasn't just Ivy Snowfall anymore, she was the heir to families who'd built the magical foundations that Winter Court authority rested on.

And she was choosing to use that heritage to ensure that no one else would be forced to trade autonomy for safety the way we'd been pressured to do.

"Are we still a team?" I asked, echoing our conversation from what felt like a lifetime ago.

"Always," she replied, and this time the word carried the weight of magical legacy that predated Winter Court politics by generations.

The bells tolled, marking the mandate's official start. Beyond the crystal panes, aurora glyphs stitched the Court's supervision order across the sky for anyone with knowledge to read them. But Ivy's fingers tightened around mine, and the medical bay's lattice hummed lower as her new geometry settled into place.

"First, Dylan and Lyra," she said. "Then the chamber."

Our binding rune answered, warm, steady, refusing to bow. The Winter Court had spent years building a cage for two children they'd marked for territorial magic.

Architects had just picked up their tools.

CHAPTER SEVENTEEN
THE ACTIVATION

IVY

Morning classes under Winter Court supervision felt like performing magic in a fishbowl.

Lady Silverleaf had taken residence at the back of Professor Meridian's Advanced Theoretical Applications classroom, her crystalline tablet documenting every collaborative spell Rowan and I attempted. Not just our magical output, our conversations, our glances, even the way we synchronized our breathing during complex castings. Everything was being recorded for analysis by people whose intentions we couldn't trust.

"Today we'll be working on adaptive ward construction," Professor Meridian announced, her voice carrying the careful neutrality she'd adopted since supervision began. "The goal is to create defensive barriers that can modify their structure in response to changing magical conditions."

Adaptive ward construction. The irony wasn't lost on me, learning to build defenses that could change according to external pressure while being watched by people whose external pressure was the reason we needed defenses in the first place.

Through our bond, I felt Rowan's mixture of frustration and determination. He'd been quieter since the supervision mandate took effect, more controlled in his responses, as if he was trying to minimize the amount of himself that Winter Court observers could document and analyze.

But underneath the careful restraint, I could sense the architectural knowledge I'd inherited making connections that hadn't been there before. The ward construction techniques Professor Meridian was teaching weren't just academic exercises, they were simplified versions of the territorial magic that my family had used to build NPU's foundational infrastructure.

"Miss Snowfall, Mr. Blackthorn," Professor Meridian continued, "please demonstrate collaborative ward construction for the class. Standard partnership protocols, beginning with individual casting and progressing to synchronized integration."

Standard partnership protocols. Which meant performing exactly the kind of magic that Lady Silverleaf was here to observe, document, and potentially manipulate for Winter Court objectives.

Rowan and I took our positions at the demonstration platform, maintaining the skin contact that our bond required while trying to ignore the way Lady Silverleaf's tablet hummed with increased recording activity. Other students had arranged themselves in a semicircle around the platform, their expressions ranging from supportive curiosity to the kind of fascination that came from watching something that might explode.

"Begin with individual ward construction," Professor Meridian instructed. "Miss Snowfall, create a basic light barrier. Mr. Blackthorn, demonstrate frost reinforcement. Then integrate according to established partnership techniques."

I called up my light magic, letting illumination flow from my palms in patterns that should have been familiar. But the moment my magic manifested, I felt the difference that inherited knowledge had made. Instead of the simple light constructs I'd been creating for weeks, my magic automatically structured itself into architectural patterns, geometric frameworks designed to support much more complex magical applications than basic ward construction.

The light barrier that emerged was beautiful, but it was also clearly beyond what any undergraduate student should have been capable of creating. Crystalline patterns that looked like captured aurora, with structural sophistication that belonged in graduate-level coursework rather than introductory partnership magic.

Through our bond, I felt Rowan's surprise at the enhanced complexity of my casting, followed by his understanding that the knowledge integration from my parents' message had fundamentally changed what I was capable of creating.

"Fascinating," Lady Silverleaf murmured from her observation position, her voice carrying satisfaction that made my stomach clench with warning. "The magical density readings are considerably higher than previous demonstrations."

Considerably higher. Which meant my enhanced abilities were exactly what she'd been hoping to document, evidence that our partnership had developed capabilities that exceeded normal student parameters.

"Mr. Blackthorn," Professor Meridian said with careful neutrality, "please add frost reinforcement to Miss Snowfall's construction."

Rowan extended his hands toward my light barrier, his frost magic responding with the precise control that had become second nature over the past few weeks. But the moment his magic interfaced with mine, something unexpected happened.

Not synchronization, seizure. Violent, involuntary connection that ripped past choice and slammed our magical cores together with overwhelming force.

The ward construction exploded outward, growing from a simple defensive barrier into a complex dominion display that filled the entire classroom with aurora patterns and crystalline formations. Not just collaborative magic, control magic, the kind that established authority over specific locations.

Through our bond, I felt Rowan's alarm matching my own as we realized what was happening. Our magic wasn't just integrating, it was being compelled to demonstrate the dominion applications that made us valuable to Winter Court objectives.

"Mr. Blackthorn! Miss Snowfall!" Professor Meridian called sharply, her wind sprite magic flaring as she tried to contain the expanding magical display. "Maintain conscious control of your casting!"

But we couldn't maintain control. Whatever was forcing our bond to activate was beyond our ability to resist through willpower alone. The territorial magic continued expanding, creating dominion patterns that interfaced with NPU's foundational infrastructure in ways that should have been impossible for students to access.

"Magnificent," Lady Silverleaf breathed, rising from her observation position with obvious pleasure. "The integration is proceeding exactly as intended."

As intended. Through our bond, I felt Rowan's sharp understanding of what those words meant. This wasn't accidental magical escalation, it was deliberate activation, triggered by external intervention rather than our conscious choice.

Lady Silverleaf withdrew something from her robes that made my blood run cold with recognition. The same crystalline device she'd produced during our breakfast confrontation weeks ago, now pulsing with energy that resonated directly with our binding runes.

"Lady Silverleaf," Professor Meridian said with authority that couldn't quite mask her alarm, "please explain what you're doing to my students."

"The key shows what they really are," Lady Silverleaf replied with chilling satisfaction. "Properly guided, of course."

Conscious resistance. Which meant they'd been waiting for an opportunity to override our choices, to force our bond to display capabilities that we might not have been willing to demonstrate voluntarily.

The territorial magic continued expanding, and through our connection, I felt Rowan fighting to regain control of his frost magic as it responded to compulsions that originated from the activation key rather than his conscious direction. His storm magic was spiking toward the destructive patterns that characterized the Blackthorn curse, but instead of the chaotic violence that usually resulted from loss of control, the external activation was channeling his power into structured applications.

"The readings are approaching dangerous levels," Dylan called from his monitoring station, where he and Lyra were tracking magical density fluctuations that exceeded safe parameters for classroom demonstrations. "Professor Meridian, we need to terminate this exercise immediately."

"I agree," Professor Meridian said firmly, moving toward Lady Silverleaf with protective authority. "Deactivate whatever you're using to manipulate their magical output."

"The demonstration is proceeding within acceptable parameters," Lady Silverleaf replied smoothly, though I could see satisfaction in her pale eyes as our territorial magic continued to interface with NPU's infrastructure. "Surely the university wants to understand the full extent of what partnership magic can accomplish when properly guided."

Properly guided. The euphemism for forced compliance made my inherited architectural knowledge flare with indignation. This wasn't guidance, it was magical assault disguised as academic observation.

But even as I fought against the external activation, part of me was learning from what was being forced to happen. The territorial magic that Lady Silverleaf was compelling us to demonstrate wasn't just random displays of power, it was systematic modification of NPU's foundational infrastructure, designed to establish Winter Court control over magical systems that my family had built centuries ago.

Through our bond, I felt Rowan's understanding of the same thing. They weren't just testing our capabilities, they were using our connection to my architectural heritage to gain access to magical systems that had been designed to resist Winter Court political control.

The device pulsed brighter, and suddenly the forced connection deepened beyond anything we'd experienced during normal binding integration. Not just magical synchronization, but consciousness merger.

I felt Rowan's mind bloom open to mine like a flower to sunlight, his memories, his fears, the careful control he maintained over storm magic that wanted to destroy everything he cared about. For a heartbeat, I experienced eighteen years of loneliness from the inside, the weight of carrying magic that everyone expected to turn deadly.

Then he was in my mind just as completely, feeling three years of deliberate invisibility, the exhaustion of making yourself small, the terror of being seen and found wanting. Our memories intertwined, creating understanding deeper than words.

And through that enhanced connection, I felt something else. His storm magic wasn't just responding to external compulsion, it was drawing on the architectural knowledge I'd inherited, using my family's magical techniques to give his frost power structural applications that exceeded traditional Blackthorn capabilities.

We're both being changed, I realized with growing alarm. *The activation isn't just forcing us to demonstrate what we can already do, it's using our bond to transfer capabilities between us.*

Through our shared consciousness, I felt Rowan's agreement, along with his recognition that whatever was happening to us was irreversible. The knowledge transfer that had begun with my parents' message was now extending to him through forced magical integration, giving him access to architectural understanding that would fundamentally change what his magic could accomplish.

But if we can both access architectural knowledge, his thoughts came through our enhanced connection with crystal clarity, *then we can use it to resist what they're trying to do.*

He was right. The same forced activation that was compelling us to demonstrate territorial magic was also giving us the knowledge necessary to understand how that magic functioned. And understanding how it functioned meant understanding how to modify it according to our own intentions rather than external compulsion.

I reached deeper into the architectural inheritance that connected me to NPU's foundational systems, but instead of allowing the territorial magic to establish Winter Court dominion, I began modifying the patterns according to my own design intentions.

The aurora displays that filled the classroom shifted from Winter Court heraldry into something entirely new, geometric patterns that represented partnership chosen rather than control imposed, collaborative magic that enhanced individual autonomy rather than subsuming it into external authority structures.

Through our bond, I felt Rowan understanding what I was attempting, and his frost magic began supporting my modifications with structural reinforcement that made the new patterns stable and resistant to external manipulation.

"What are they doing?" Lady Silverleaf demanded, her voice sharp with alarm as she realized that our demonstration was no longer following the script that her activation key was designed to enforce.

"They're showing you what partnership magic actually accomplishes when it's not being manipulated by people who don't understand it," Professor Meridian replied with satisfaction that suggested she'd been hoping for exactly this kind of development.

The territorial magic that filled the classroom wasn't establishing Winter Court control over NPU's infrastructure, it was reinforcing the university's independence by strengthening magical systems that predated court political authority. Instead of dominion, we were creating sanctuary. Instead of control, we were building protection.

Lady Silverleaf's activation key began sparking with unstable energy as the forced bond responded to our modifications by rejecting external manipulation entirely. The crystalline device was designed to compel demonstration of territorial magic that served Winter Court objectives, not architectural applications that protected academic independence.

"Terminate the activation," Professor Meridian commanded with authority that brooked no argument. "You're endangering my students with magical technology that's clearly malfunctioning."

"The technology is functioning exactly as designed," Lady

Silverleaf insisted, though I could see growing concern in her expression as the activation key's energy patterns became increasingly erratic. "The binding is simply displaying more sophisticated capabilities than initial assessments predicted."

More sophisticated capabilities. Through our enhanced connection, I felt Rowan's grim amusement at the understatement. We weren't just displaying capabilities, we were actively rejecting the political framework that Winter Court authority depended on, using our forced demonstration to prove that partnership magic could challenge territorial dominion rather than serving it.

The activation key pulsed one final time, then cracked as the energy patterns it was designed to control shifted beyond its ability to maintain influence. The forced bond activation didn't terminate, it transformed, becoming voluntary partnership enhanced by conscious choice rather than external compulsion.

The territorial magic that filled the classroom settled into stable patterns that felt both ancient and perfectly suited to current needs. Not Winter Court dominion, but NPU independence. Not political control, but academic sanctuary.

"Extraordinary," Dylan breathed from his monitoring station, studying readings that showed magical integration at levels that exceeded anything in partnership magic literature. "Your bond just rejected external control while maintaining enhanced capabilities. That shouldn't be theoretically possible."

"It's possible because partnership magic is fundamentally about choice," I said, my voice carrying the confidence of someone who'd just discovered that inherited knowledge included not just architectural techniques, but the philosophical principles that governed their application. "When you try to force people to demonstrate capabilities against their will, you're not seeing partnership magic, you're seeing magical assault."

Lady Silverleaf stared at her broken activation key with an

expression that mixed frustration with grudging respect. "The binding has developed beyond initial parameters," she admitted with diplomatic language that couldn't quite disguise her alarm. "Further observation will be required to assess the full implications."

"Further observation will be conducted according to academic protocols that respect student autonomy," Professor Meridian replied firmly. "No more unauthorized activation of magical devices in my classroom."

But even as Lady Silverleaf withdrew her damaged equipment and made notes about the unexpected development, I could feel through our enhanced bond that this confrontation had changed something fundamental about our situation.

We were no longer just students whose magical development was being monitored by external authority. We were partners whose combined capabilities had proven resistant to political manipulation, whose territorial magic could challenge Winter Court dominion rather than serving it.

And that made us considerably more dangerous to existing power structures than anyone had anticipated.

"Are you both alright?" Lyra asked with genuine concern as the territorial magic displays faded and the classroom returned to something resembling normal.

"Better than alright," Rowan replied, his voice carrying certainty that came from shared understanding of what we'd just accomplished. "We just learned that our partnership is stronger than the people trying to control it."

Through our bond, I felt the truth of his words resonating with architectural knowledge that now belonged to both of us. The forced activation had been intended to demonstrate Winter Court control over our capabilities.

Instead, it had proven that some partnerships were more powerful than the political frameworks designed to contain them.

"What happens next?" I asked Professor Meridian quietly, noting the way other students were still staring at the residual aurora patterns that decorated the classroom walls.

"Next, we document what just occurred and ensure that it never happens again without your explicit consent," she replied with protective authority. "Partnership magic demonstrations will continue, but under academic supervision rather than external manipulation."

I could feel that both Rowan and I understood the larger implications of what had just taken place. The Winter Court's patience with observation and documentation was clearly running out. Lady Silverleaf's attempt to force demonstration of our capabilities suggested that more direct intervention would follow if they couldn't find other ways to ensure our compliance with their objectives.

And now that our bond had proven capable of rejecting external control while maintaining enhanced capabilities, the stakes of that intervention had just increased dramatically.

Whatever came next, we'd face it with architectural knowledge that belonged to both of us, territorial magic that strengthened academic independence rather than serving political authority, and the understanding that partnership magic was most powerful when it was chosen rather than imposed.

The Winter Court had spent years developing tools to control magical partnerships.

They'd never considered that some partnerships might be strong enough to break those tools and build something better in their place.

As we gathered our materials and prepared to leave the classroom, I caught Rowan's hand in mine and felt our binding runes pulse with warm light that had nothing to do with external activation and everything to do with conscious choice.

Together? I asked through our mental connection.

Always, he replied, and the word carried the weight of architectural knowledge, enhanced capabilities, and the growing understanding that we were building something that would outlast any attempt to control it.

The aurora patterns on the classroom walls pulsed once more, as if acknowledging a partnership that had just proven itself stronger than the forces trying to shape it.

Whatever the Winter Court tried next, they'd learn what foundations built on choice could withstand, and that some partnerships ran too deep to control.

CHAPTER EIGHTEEN
FRACTURES

ROWAN

The campus didn't break at three in the morning. It remembered. And the remembering hurt.

Aurora patterns cracked the Observatory's upper dome with a resonant frequency that made sleeping impossible. The sound echoed across the residential wings like breaking glass, sharp, violent, wrong. Through our bond, I could feel Ivy's restless sleep, dreams filled with architectural knowledge still organizing itself into usable understanding.

From my window, I watched students emerge from dormitories in pajamas and robes, their faces turned upward toward the fractured crystal overhead. Some pointed at the jagged aurora light bleeding through the cracks. Others backed away with the instinctive wariness of people who'd learned that magical accidents on this scale usually meant someone was in serious trouble.

"Is that supposed to happen?" I heard a first-year sprite ask her roommate as they stood in the snow-covered courtyard below.

"Nothing's supposed to happen at three AM," came the sharp reply. "Someone's lost control of something big."

Their whispers carried on the still winter air, joining dozens of similar conversations as the news spread through the residential halls. *Lost control.* If only they knew how deliberately this had been triggered, and by whom.

The forced activation had changed us both. NPU's foundation grid responded to our presence now in ways that felt both natural and deeply unsettling. We weren't just bound to each other anymore, we were bound to the place itself, to infrastructure that had been waiting eighteen years for someone with the right bloodline to wake it up.

My communication crystal chimed with Dylan's encrypted signature: *Emergency meeting, Observatory Sub-Level 3, 0400 hours. Bring Ivy. Situation developing.*

Sub-Level 3 wasn't standard campus infrastructure, it was part of the older foundations that predated Winter Court authority. The fact that Dylan knew about it suggested yesterday's magical surge had revealed more than just our enhanced capabilities.

I found Ivy already awake in the common room, standing at the window with her binding rune glowing softly through her nightclothes. She didn't turn when I approached, but through our bond, I felt her awareness of my presence.

"The whole north wing is talking about us," she said quietly. "They think we broke something."

"Did we?"

"We fixed something." Her voice carried the certainty of inherited knowledge, but underneath it, I caught the tremor of someone who was beginning to understand the magnitude of what we'd accidentally awakened. "The question is whether anyone else will see it that way."

As we made our way through campus toward the Observatory, the building welcomed us like family returning home. Corridor lights lifted ahead of us with a gentle aurora glow. Sealed passages from earlier centuries split open at Ivy's approach, revealing shortcuts through foundation levels that most faculty didn't know existed. The air warmed around us, adjusting to our baseline body temperature with the kind of thoughtful hospitality usually reserved for honored guests.

Other students we passed in the corridors gave us wide berths, their conversations dying as we approached and resuming in urgent whispers once we'd moved on. I caught fragments of speculation that ranged from awed to frightened:

", heard they can control the whole campus infrastructure now..."

", dangerous, that kind of power in students..."

", my cousin at Frostbane Academy says their Winter Court connections run deep..."

", probably not even their fault, but still..."

The lattice wasn't accommodating students, it was welcoming administrators. And everyone could sense the difference.

Ivy tested the infrastructure's responsiveness as we walked, trailing her fingers along crystal panels that brightened at her touch, letting pathway stones warm beneath her feet until they glowed like captured starlight. Each response sent ripples of unease through me that had nothing to do with the magic itself and everything to do with the implications.

"The infrastructure is treating us like family," she observed as decades-sealed passages opened at her approach.

"Your family did build most of this," I reminded her, though through our bond, I felt her growing awareness that inherited privilege came with inherited responsibility she'd never chosen.

"Not just family," she said softly, pausing as an ornate doorway carved with Lux and Niveus heraldry responded to her presence with patterns of light that spelled out *Welcome home* in scripts older than the Winter Court itself. "Heirs."

The word hung between us like a promise and a threat. Through our connection, I felt her mixture of awe and terror at discovering she wasn't just Ivy Snowfall anymore, she was someone whose magical signature could wake infrastructure that had been sleeping for nearly two decades, whose architectural knowledge gave her administrative access to systems that formed the foundation of northern territorial authority.

Sub-Level 3 was a testament to magical engineering that predated modern academic architecture by several centuries. Crystalline corridors carved from living ice stretched into depths I couldn't calculate, illuminated by aurora patterns that provided steady light without external power sources. The air here felt older, more fundamental, like breathing the magical atmosphere that had existed before Winter Court politics had complicated simple collaboration with territorial authority.

The walls themselves told stories in architectural flourishes that spoke to centuries of magical development. Runes carved by sprite-light into crystalline surfaces recorded collaborative spells that had shaped the northern territories. Ice formations that captured and held emotional resonance still hummed with the satisfaction of builders who'd created something beautiful and functional. Even the pathway stones remembered the footsteps of architects who'd designed this place as sanctuary rather than fortress.

Compared to the sharp elegance of Winter Court administrative buildings I'd visited as a child, Sub-Level 3 felt warm despite being carved from ice. Where court architecture emphasized dominance and control, this place had been designed for collaboration and discovery. The difference was subtle but profound, like comparing a cage to a garden.

Dylan and Lyra were waiting in a circular meeting chamber, surrounded by displays showing real-time magical readings from across campus. Professor Meridian stood near the central console, wind sprite magic creating pine-scented air currents that carried the comfort of ancient forests. Professor Blitzen occupied a crystalline chair that sparked gently when she moved, her electrical aura responding to some deep tension in the magical atmosphere. Near the entrance, Marcus Thornfield sat with careful attention, student liaison from the Ward Guild, documenting everything for the emergency log with the methodical precision of someone who understood that tonight's decisions would have lasting consequences.

Through our bond, I felt Ivy noting how the crystalline surfaces responded to her presence with subtle brightening, acknowledging her inherited authority even as she struggled to understand what that authority meant.

"Campus-wide magical destabilization," Lyra said without preamble, gesturing toward displays that showed aurora patterns spanning a geographic area far larger than NPU's immediate grounds. "The integration you achieved yesterday created resonance patterns interfacing with magical systems throughout the northern territories."

Her academic excitement was tempered by visible concern as she adjusted the displays to reveal the full scope of what we'd accidentally triggered. "Forty-seven confirmed awakenings, including the Court's administrative spine."

I felt Ivy's shock ripple through me like a physical impact. We hadn't just challenged Winter Court oversight, we'd accidentally triggered awakening across infrastructure that formed the foundation of their territorial control. The binding rune on my ribs pulsed with shared alarm as the implications settled between us.

We didn't mean for this to happen. Her mental voice carried the bewildered distress of someone discovering that their personal choices had massive political consequences.

I know, I replied, trying to anchor her growing panic with steadiness I wasn't sure I felt. *But meaning to or not, we need to deal with what is rather than what we intended.*

"Your ancestors were the primary architectural contractors for dominion grids throughout the northern territories," Marcus said quietly, his careful documentation of our expressions suggesting he was logging emotional responses as well as factual information. "When they fled court politics eighteen years ago, they took technical knowledge that no one else possessed. Knowledge that's been sleeping in infrastructure installations across the region, waiting for someone with the right bloodline to wake it up."

Professor Blitzen's chair sparked more brightly as electrical tension made the chamber's surfaces glow with contained energy. "The question is whether the awakening was accidental or deliberately triggered by someone who's been waiting for the right moment to challenge Winter Court territorial authority."

"The awakening patterns aren't random," Lyra continued, adjusting displays to reveal something that made my blood chill. "Someone with detailed Lux/Niveus knowledge is using yesterday's trigger to activate specific installations in sequence."

The map on her display wasn't a random activation. It was a crown-arc, a maintenance path that swept from the coast inward, node by sleeping node, the way you wake a frozen river without flooding the banks. The kind of systematic technical procedure that required both architectural expertise and political strategy.

"My parents," Ivy whispered, her voice carrying the hollow

shock of someone realizing they'd been a catalyst in a plan they'd never been told about. "They're using yesterday's activation to access systems they haven't been able to reach for eighteen years."

Through our bond, I felt her mixture of betrayal and understanding. Her parents had spent eighteen years protecting her from Winter Court attention, but they'd also been preparing for this moment, when their daughter's inherited capabilities could be used to challenge the political authority that had forced them into exile.

"To prove that Winter Court territorial authority is built on foundations they don't control," I said, understanding the larger game with the kind of political clarity that came from growing up in a family where strategy and survival were often the same thing. "If your family can demonstrate that their architectural knowledge still supersedes court political claims, then every installation becomes negotiable rather than sovereign."

Professor Meridian's wind sprite magic created subtle air currents that carried tension like approaching storm-weather. "The Winter Court will perceive this as a direct challenge to their fundamental authority. Not academic disagreement, but existential threat."

"Estimated completion time?" Professor Blitzen asked, electrical tension making the chamber's surfaces glow with contained lightning.

"Seventy-two hours to finish the crown-arc pattern," Lyra replied grimly, her academic precision doing nothing to soften the alarming implications. "Or to stop it."

Through our bond, I felt Ivy's architectural knowledge providing context that transformed fear into determination. The crown-arc pattern wasn't just a political demonstration, it was infrastructure restoration, awakening systems that had been designed to serve educational collaboration rather than territorial control. Her family wasn't trying to destroy Winter Court authority so much as they were trying to remind the magical world that other forms of governance were possible.

They're trying to give us a choice, she realized through our connection. *Between serving political authority or educational mission.*

And the Winter Court is going to do everything in their power to ensure we don't get that choice, I replied, my own political experience providing understanding of what always happened when existing power structures felt threatened.

"What kind of direct action are we anticipating?" I asked, though I suspected I already knew the answer.

"The kind that doesn't distinguish between students and political threats," Marcus said quietly, his understanding of court politics providing context that academic perspectives couldn't match. "If the Winter Court perceives that their territorial authority is being challenged through technical means they can't control, they'll respond with whatever force they consider necessary to preserve their power base."

The words hit both Ivy and me through our bond like physical blows. Through our enhanced connection, I felt her growing understanding that we were no longer just students whose magical development had political implications. We were potentially the catalyst for confrontation between different approaches to territorial governance, educational collaboration versus political control.

And the Winter Court's preferred method of dealing with catalysts they couldn't control was elimination.

"We need allies," Ivy said with architectural understanding that provided strategic as well as technical insight. "If this is going to become a confrontation between different approaches to territorial authority, we need people who understand that magical infrastructure should serve educational rather than political objectives."

Professor Meridian's expression carried the weight of someone who'd spent decades watching political forces try to subordinate academic independence to external control. "Agreed. But we also need to understand exactly what your family is trying to accomplish through the activation sequence. Are they seeking to negotiate with Winter Court authority, or are they planning to challenge it directly?"

Before anyone could respond, the chamber's communication system activated with aurora patterns that I recognized as emergency priority routing. The crystalline surfaces around us hummed with harmonics that spoke of urgent messages transmitted through infrastructure that predated normal communication channels.

The message that materialized was brief, formal, and utterly terrifying in its implications:

University Administration: Winter Court Delegation requests immediate conference regarding territorial authority clarification. Delegation includes Lord Darian Frostborn, Lady Silverleaf, Court Architectural Assessor, and Magical Infrastructure Security Division. Estimated arrival: 0800 hours. Purpose: Resolution of architectural activation anomalies through diplomatic or alternative means. Academic Affairs.

Diplomatic or alternative means. The kind of political language that meant negotiation would be offered, but compliance would be enforced regardless of university preferences.

Through our bond, I felt Ivy's spike of terror at seeing my uncle's name in official capacity, followed by her determination not to let fear paralyze her when decisive action was needed. Her binding rune pulsed with warmth that anchored my own storm magic before it could spiral toward the destructive patterns that characterized the Blackthorn curse under pressure.

"Four hours," Professor Blitzen observed with electrical tension that made the chamber's crystalline surfaces glow with contained energy. "To prepare for a confrontation that could determine whether NPU maintains academic independence or becomes subject to Winter Court direct administration."

Marcus's stylus moved faster across his documentation tablet, recording not just the facts but the emotional undercurrents that would help the Ward Guild understand what they were potentially defending against. Through our bond, I felt Ivy's gratitude for his presence, someone whose political understanding matched the magnitude of what we were facing.

"Magical Infrastructure Security Division," Lyra said with academic precision that couldn't quite mask her alarm. "That's not diplomatic oversight. That's enforcement capacity designed to neutralize threats to territorial stability."

Through our bond, I felt Ivy's architectural knowledge providing understanding of what Winter Court direct administration would mean, not just for our partnership, but for every aspect of magical education. Technical knowledge subordinated to political objectives. Infrastructure designed to serve territorial authority rather than academic excellence. Students trained to support existing power structures rather than developing capabilities that might challenge them.

The vision of NPU transformed from sanctuary into an indoctrination center hit both of us through our connection with the force of shared nightmare. Not just the end of our partnership, but the death of everything the university was supposed to represent.

They can't have this place, Ivy's mental voice carried the fierce protectiveness of someone whose family had built something beautiful and refused to watch it be corrupted. *Whatever it costs, whatever we have to do, they can't turn this into another tool for polit-ical control.*

Agreed, I replied, letting my own resolve flow through our connection to anchor her determination. *But we need to be smart about how we fight them. Direct confrontation plays to their strengths.*

"We fight," Ivy said aloud with certainty that came from inherited knowledge of what her family had been trying to preserve for eighteen years. "We use the architectural advantage we have, we rally everyone who believes that magical education should serve students rather than political authorities, and we prove that some foundations are too strong to be controlled by people who didn't build them."

Her voice carried the confidence of someone who'd just real-ized that inherited knowledge included not just technical capabil-ities, but the philosophical framework that governed their application. Not just how to build infrastructure, but why it should be built to serve collaboration rather than control.

"Together?" I asked, echoing the conversation that had started our partnership weeks ago.

"Always," she replied, and the word carried the weight of territorial magic, architectural knowledge, and the growing understanding that we were building something that would outlast any attempt to control it.

The displays around us pulsed with aurora patterns that showed magical awakening across installations throughout the northern territories, a network of power that predated Winter Court political authority and could potentially replace it with something designed to serve magical education rather than terri-torial control.

I felt the moment when our shared resolve crystallized into something that felt less like defiance and more like destiny. We weren't just fighting for our partnership anymore. We were fighting for the future of magical education itself.

Whatever the Winter Court delegation brought with them in four hours, they'd discover that some partnerships were strong enough to change the foundations on which that political authority rested.

And some students were ready to build a better future, even if it meant challenging everyone who profited from the current one.

CHAPTER NINETEEN
CHOOSING SIDES

IVY

The Winter Court delegation arrived at exactly eight o'clock, because punctuality was apparently a form of intimidation when you commanded enough magical authority to make entire universities rearrange their schedules around your convenience.

I watched from the Observatory's upper viewing platform as three crystalline sleighs descended from the aurora-streaked sky, each one carved from ice so pure it seemed to bend light around itself. Silver runners traced with aurora patterns left shimmering trails in the air, while banners bearing the interlocked snowflakes of Winter Court authority snapped in winds that carried the scent of distant storms. The sleighs landed with ceremonial precision on NPU's main courtyard, their passengers emerging in robes that made the morning air shimmer with contained frost magic.

Lord Darian stepped down first, his pale hair catching the morning light like spun frost, every movement radiating the kind of authority that came from centuries of noble breeding. His court robes bore rank insignia that marked him as more than just a family, territorial administrator, with legal standing to command rather than request. Lady Silverleaf followed, her winter-white cloak fastened with pins that pulsed with contained magic, while two figures I didn't recognize flanked them in the kind of formal formation that spoke to military rather than diplomatic protocol.

"Magical Infrastructure Security Division," Rowan said quietly beside me, his voice carrying the flat recognition of someone who'd grown up understanding exactly what that title meant. "They brought enforcement."

I felt his mixture of fear and protective fury as he watched his uncle stride across NPU's main courtyard with the confidence of someone who owned whatever ground he walked on. The binding rune on my wrist pulsed with sympathetic tension, our magical signatures automatically synchronizing to provide stability against the political pressure we both knew was coming.

"Students are gathering," Dylan observed from his position near the platform's edge, where crystalline barriers provided a clear view of campus activity. "Word's spread about the delegation."

He was right. Clusters of students had emerged from dormitories and academic buildings, but they weren't arranging themselves randomly. Near the Administrative Tower, a group of upperclassmen had gathered around a hastily erected banner reading "Academic Independence Now!" Their voices carried across the courtyard in rhythmic chants: "Our magic, our choice! Our campus, our voice!"

But closer to the Winter Court delegation, another crowd had formed with notably different energy. Signs reading "Stability Through Structure" and "Honor Court Authority" suggested these students viewed the envoys' presence as welcome oversight rather than threatening intrusion. Frost Silverleaf moved among them with her mother's graceful authority, distributing pamphlets that bore the Winter Court crest.

"Campus is splitting," Professor Meridian said grimly as she joined us on the viewing platform, her wind sprite magic creating pine-scented air currents that carried tension like approaching storm-weather. "Some students believe Winter Court oversight would provide stability. Others see it as the end of academic independence."

Through our bond, I felt Rowan's understanding of what that split meant for our situation. We weren't just facing political pressure from external authorities anymore, we were becoming symbols in a campus-wide debate about whether magical education should serve institutional independence or territorial authority.

Between the two main groups, smaller clusters of undecided students watched the growing demonstration with obvious uncertainty. I caught fragments of worried conversations:

", heard Professor Ember say the Court's just trying to help..."

", but what if they're wrong? What if this is about control?"

", look how organized Silverleaf's people are. Someone's been planning this..."

"Faculty council convenes in two hours," Professor Meridian continued, her voice carrying the weight of someone who'd spent the night arguing with colleagues whose positions were hardening around irreconcilable differences. "Formal vote on whether to comply with Winter Court demands for immediate custody, or maintain university independence regardless of consequences."

Immediate custody. The euphemism hit both of us through our connection like physical blows. Not supervision or oversight, possession.

"What are the likely outcomes?" I asked, though I wasn't sure I wanted to know the answer.

"Split vote," Professor Meridian admitted with frustrated honesty. "Ember's faction believes compliance is the only way to prevent escalation that could endanger the entire campus. My faction believes that surrendering students to external political authority violates everything NPU was founded to protect."

I caught Rowan's memory of overhearing Professor Ember in the faculty lounge yesterday, her voice carrying the kind of certainty that brooked no disagreement: "Sometimes protecting students means making difficult choices they're too young to understand. The Winter Court isn't our enemy, they're offering guidance we'd be foolish to refuse."

"And if it's a split vote?" Rowan asked.

"Then Chancellor Northwind casts the deciding ballot," Professor Meridian replied. "And she's been notably absent from preliminary discussions."

Through our bond, I felt Rowan's spike of alarm. In Winter Court politics, notable absence usually meant someone was negotiating private arrangements that wouldn't survive public scrutiny. The kind of behind-closed-doors deals that transformed public votes into predetermined outcomes.

"There are rumors she's been in communication with Court representatives since before the delegation officially arrived," Professor Meridian added quietly. "Whether that represents compromise or collaboration remains unclear."

"We should prepare for both outcomes," I said, my voice steadier than I felt. "Compliance and resistance."

"Agreed," Professor Meridian nodded. "But there's something else you need to understand about your current magical state. The bond integration has progressed beyond anything documented in partnership magic literature."

She gestured toward monitoring displays that Dylan and Lyra had been maintaining since yesterday's forced activation. The readings showed magical synchronization so complete that our individual signatures were becoming impossible to distinguish.

"Separation beyond fifteen minutes would now result in magical collapse for both of you," Lyra said with clinical precision that couldn't soften the devastating implications. "Complete failure of your individual magical cores."

The words hit me like ice water. I felt Rowan absorbing the same information with a mixture of horror and protective determination. But underneath his immediate reaction, I caught something else, the same strange relief I was experiencing.

One magical entity in two bodies. The phrase should have been terrifying. Instead, it felt like confirmation of something I'd been sensing but hadn't been able to name. The growing awareness that being separate from Rowan was becoming not just uncomfortable, but fundamentally wrong. Like trying to breathe with only one lung or think with half a brain.

Was that loss of individual identity, or evolution into something better than either of us could be alone? Through our bond, I felt Rowan wrestling with the same question, the fear that we were losing ourselves, warring with the certainty that what we were becoming together exceeded anything we'd been apart.

"How long do we have before that becomes irreversible?" Rowan asked.

"It may already be irreversible," Lyra admitted. "But if the integration continues at current rates, within seventy-two hours your magical signatures will be so intertwined that you'll essentially be one magical entity in two bodies."

The timeline should have felt like a countdown to catastrophe. Instead, through our bond, I felt something that might have been anticipation. Whatever political forces were trying to tear us apart, our magic itself was choosing integration over separation.

"Is that necessarily bad?" I asked quietly.

"It's unprecedented," Lyra replied. "But the readings suggest that rather than diminishing your individual capabilities, the integration is creating something fundamentally new. Not just enhanced partnership magic, but collaborative consciousness that exceeds the sum of its parts."

I felt Rowan's understanding of what she meant. The mental connection we'd developed wasn't just emotional support or magical communication, it was evolving into shared awareness that made us stronger together than either of us had ever been alone.

"Like the architectural consciousness I inherited," I realized aloud. "But applied to personal relationships rather than infrastructure management."

"Exactly," Dylan said with the kind of academic excitement that suggested he was documenting developments that would reshape partnership magic theory for generations. "You're pioneering collaborative magic that could fundamentally change how we understand individual versus shared magical identity."

But before anyone could explore the implications further, the Observatory's communication system activated with priority routing that carried Winter Court authority.

University Administration: Immediate conference requested with subjects Rowan Blackthorn and Ivy Snowfall. Location: Administrative Tower, Conference Room 1. Time: 0930 hours. Attendance required. Refusal will be interpreted as non-compliance with territorial authority. Winter Court Delegation.

Attendance required. Not requested, commanded.

I could feel Rowan's careful analysis of the summons, along with his growing certainty that this wasn't just another interview. The Winter Court had moved beyond observation and documentation to direct action.

"They're not asking anymore," he said quietly.

"No," Professor Meridian agreed. "They're asserting authority they believe supersedes university independence."

"Do we have legal grounds to refuse?" I asked.

"Legal grounds, yes," Professor Meridian replied with grim honesty. "Practical ability to enforce those grounds against Winter Court political pressure? That remains to be seen."

The viewing platform's crystal barriers hummed with harmonic resonance as magical tension spread across campus. Through our bond, I could feel the way NPU's infrastructure was responding to my presence, not just accommodation, but active support. The architectural consciousness I'd inherited recognized the political threat to educational independence and was prepared to defend against it.

"The campus lattice is rallying," I said with growing certainty. "Whatever my family built into NPU's foundations, it's designed to resist external political control."

"Infrastructure resistance won't protect you from magical enforcement," Professor Meridian warned. "If the Winter Court decides to use direct action rather than political pressure, they have capabilities that exceed anything NPU's defensive systems were designed to counter."

"Then we need to be smarter than they expect," I said, feeling resolve crystallize in my chest like structural magic finding its proper form. "Use the political framework they're operating within to limit their options for direct action."

"How?"

"By making our choice public," Rowan said with sudden understanding. "If we openly declare that we're choosing each other rather than submitting to external authority, they can't frame custody as protective supervision. It becomes political kidnapping."

I felt his strategic thinking providing the tactical framework for resistance that my architectural knowledge couldn't supply alone. We weren't just building defenses, we were constructing a political position that would be harder for the Winter Court to attack without revealing their true objectives.

"Public declaration during faculty council session," I added, understanding his strategy. "Force them to argue their position in front of witnesses who represent academic rather than political interests."

"Risky," Professor Meridian observed. "If the vote goes against you, public defiance could be interpreted as rebellion rather than academic freedom."

"And if we don't take the risk, we lose any chance to influence the outcome," Rowan replied with the kind of political clarity that came from growing up in a family where survival often depended on understanding how power operated behind polite facades.

Through our bond, I felt his mixture of fear and determination, along with his growing realization that this confrontation had always been inevitable. The Winter Court hadn't spent years engineering our binding so they could ignore its political implications. They'd been waiting for the right moment to assert control over magical capabilities that could challenge their territorial authority.

"Conference Room 1 in thirty minutes," Dylan reminded us, checking chronometer displays that showed time passing with relentless precision. "Whatever strategy you choose, you need to decide quickly."

I looked at Rowan, noting the way morning light caught the sharp angles of his face and made his pale eyes seem to hold depths of winter magic that could reshape the world if properly directed. Through our bond, I felt his awareness of my attention, along with his own growing certainty about what choice we needed to make.

"Together?" I asked, echoing the conversation that had begun our partnership and sustained it through every challenge we'd faced.

"Always," he replied, and the word carried weight that went beyond magical binding or political necessity. "Not because we have to, but because we choose to."

The simple declaration settled something fundamental between us that had nothing to do with proximity requirements or enhanced capabilities. Whatever forces had brought us together, whatever magical integration was making separation impossible, the choice to build something meaningful from circumstance remained ours.

I felt the moment when our resolve synchronized into something that felt less like resistance and more like destiny. We weren't just defending our partnership against external control, we were choosing to become something new, something that belonged to us rather than the people who thought they could use us for their own objectives.

The Observatory's communication system chimed again, this time with an encrypted message that carried Professor Blitzen's electrical signature:

Faculty council emergency session moved to the Main Auditorium due to student attendance requests. Public gallery authorized. Vote scheduled for 1100 hours. Suggest you prepare for a campus-wide audience. Administrative Affairs.

Public gallery authorized. Which meant our declaration wouldn't just be witnessed by faculty members, it would be observed by hundreds of students whose opinions would shape the future of magical education at NPU.

"Campus-wide audience," Rowan said with a mixture of anticipation and alarm. "No taking it back once we've committed publicly."

"Good," I replied, feeling the architectural consciousness provide certainty that came from understanding the difference between buildings designed to serve temporary political convenience and those meant to last for generations. "Some choices should be permanent."

I felt his agreement resonating with determination that had nothing to do with magical compulsion and everything to do with a conscious choice to defend something worth preserving.

We had twenty-five minutes to prepare for a confrontation that would determine not just our individual futures, but the future of partnership magic and educational independence at North Pole University.

Whatever the Winter Court brought to that confrontation, they'd discover that some bonds were stronger than the political frameworks designed to control them.

And some students were ready to choose their own destiny, regardless of who preferred they remain passive subjects of other people's authority.

The aurora patterns above campus shifted into configurations that looked suspiciously like architectural blueprints, not just magical display, but instructional geometry that suggested the infrastructure itself was preparing to support whatever choice we made.

Time to find out whether foundations built on collaboration could withstand political pressure designed to transform sanctuary into submission.

But first, we had a Winter Court delegation to face. And a choice to make public that would change everything about how magical partnership was understood and practiced.

Twenty-three minutes until Conference Room 1.

Twenty-three minutes to prepare for the conversation that

would determine whether we faced the future as free partners or political assets.

The binding rune on my wrist pulsed with steady light that had nothing to do with external authority and everything to do with conscious choice.

Time to show the Winter Court what partnership magic looked like when it was defended by people who refused to be controlled.

CHAPTER TWENTY
DEFIANCE

ROWAN

Conference Room 1 had been transformed into something that resembled a court chamber more than an academic meeting space.

The usual comfortable seating had been replaced with formal arrangements that emphasized hierarchy, Winter Court representatives at the head table, university faculty in secondary positions, and Ivy and me seated at what amounted to a defendant's dock. Crystal recording devices hummed along the walls, documenting every word for analysis by people whose intentions we couldn't trust. A sealed travel sigil case sat beside the head table, its silver clasps gleaming with the kind of permanent enchantment that suggested immediate deployment.

Administrative Affairs had authorized the reconfiguration under pressure, though Chancellor Northwind's continued absence meant no one quite knew who was making decisions that should have required her direct approval.

Lord Darian sat with the kind of casual authority that made it clear he considered this his territory regardless of whose campus we were actually on. Lady Silverleaf flanked him with predatory patience, while the Court Architectural Assessor, a woman whose magical signature felt like frozen mathematics, studied blueprints that definitely hadn't come from NPU's public architectural records. She didn't look up when we entered, her lips moving in silent calculation: "Three constraints. Two thresholds. One acceptable outcome."

"Mr. Blackthorn," Lord Darian said with the false warmth that had characterized our family interactions since my parents' deaths. "Miss Snowfall. Thank you for making time in your academic schedule."

The polite fiction that this was voluntary made my storm magic coil defensively in my chest. I felt Ivy's answering spike of indignation, her light magic automatically stabilizing my frost before it could turn destructive.

"Uncle," I replied with equally false courtesy. "I understand the Winter Court has concerns about our educational arrangements."

"Concerns, yes," Lady Silverleaf interjected smoothly. "But also opportunities for mutually beneficial collaboration."

Mutually beneficial collaboration. The euphemism for forced compliance that preserved the illusion of choice while eliminating actual options.

Professor Blitzen sat with the rest of NPU's faculty representation, her silver hair crackling with electrical tension that suggested she was prepared to intervene if this meeting moved beyond diplomatic boundaries. Professor Meridian maintained careful wind sprite neutrality, though I could see from her expression that she was documenting every political nuance for later academic analysis.

"The integration you've achieved represents remarkable

magical development," the Court Architectural Assessor said, consulting readings on a crystalline tablet that pulsed with data I didn't recognize. "Particularly given the... unusual circumstances that initiated your binding."

"Unusual circumstances," Ivy repeated with deceptive casualness. "You mean the cursed charm that was planted in my Advanced Magical Applications lab?"

Silence pressed in. A recorder crystal popped, overloading, and Professor Blitzen's fingers webbed with pale lightning. I could feel Ivy's satisfaction at having broken the taboo that everyone had been dancing around, they'd experimented on us without consent, and she was done pretending otherwise.

"The charm that initiated your connection was indeed... deliberately placed," Lady Silverleaf confirmed with satisfaction that suggested she'd been waiting for the right moment to make this admission. "As part of a comprehensive evaluation of partnership magic potential among students with compatible bloodlines."

The nearest crystal flared, catching three simultaneous gasps from faculty members who were just now understanding the scope of what had been done on their campus. Professor Blitzen's lightning ticked faster, dangerous sparks building between her fingers.

Comprehensive evaluation. They'd been testing multiple student pairs, using our campus as a breeding ground for magical partnerships that could be controlled for political purposes.

"How many other students?" Professor Blitzen asked, lightning beginning to dance between her fingers. "The consent board will convene immediately to review unauthorized experimentation protocols."

"Several promising combinations were identified," the Court Architectural Assessor replied with clinical detachment, her counting never stopping: "Fourteen pairs. Seven successful bindings. Two with territorial applications." "Though Mr. Blackthorn and Miss Snowfall proved uniquely responsive to integration."

I felt Ivy's mixture of horror and fury as she realized we weren't just victims of political manipulation, we were success stories in a larger program designed to create magical partnerships that could be weaponized for Winter Court objectives.

"You used NPU students as experimental subjects without consent or institutional knowledge," Professor Meridian said, her wind sprite magic creating subtle air currents that carried the sharp scent of approaching storms.

"We evaluated students whose magical development suggested potential for applications that could benefit the entire northern territorial region," Lord Darian corrected with diplomatic language that transformed violation into virtue. "The results have exceeded our most optimistic projections."

He gestured toward displays that showed magical readings from yesterday's forced activation, along with infrastructure awakening patterns that extended far beyond NPU's immediate grounds.

"The territorial magic you demonstrated connects to installations throughout the Winter Court's sphere of influence," he continued with growing satisfaction. "With proper guidance, your partnership could provide unprecedented efficiency for magical infrastructure that currently requires costly maintenance and oversight."

You want the two of us hard-wired to your grid, human relays you can route from a throne, I thought grimly, understanding the full scope of their intentions.

"And if we prefer not to provide that kind of guidance?" I asked, though I suspected I already knew the answer. Through our bond, I felt Ivy's awareness of time passing, we'd been apart for nearly ten minutes already, our binding runes beginning their familiar low-level warning pulse.

"Then you would be choosing to deny your remarkable capabilities to people who could benefit from them," Lady Silverleaf replied with the kind of moral authority that made selfishness synonymous with refusing to serve Winter Court interests. "A waste of potential that could be seen as irresponsible, given the scope of what you could accomplish."

The trap was beautifully constructed. Either we agreed to become magical administrators for Winter Court territorial systems, or we were selfish students who cared more about personal autonomy than public service.

But through our bond, I felt Ivy's architectural consciousness providing understanding that transformed the political framework they were trying to impose. The infrastructure they wanted us to manage hadn't been designed to serve Winter Court authority, it had been built by her family to serve educational collaboration and magical innovation. Using our capabilities to restore those systems to their original purpose would strengthen academic independence rather than supporting territorial control.

"What kind of guidance are you proposing?" Ivy asked with deceptive interest.

"Residence at Winter Court for the remainder of your academic program," Lord Darian said immediately, his eagerness to secure our compliance overriding diplomatic caution. "Specialized instruction in territorial magic applications, with full court resources supporting your continued development."

"Specialized instruction by whom?" Professor Blitzen asked sharply.

"Court specialists with centuries of experience in magical administration," the Court Architectural Assessor replied.

"Knowledge that far exceeds anything available through traditional academic channels."

I felt Ivy's understanding of what that meant. Not education, but indoctrination, designed to ensure that our capabilities served established power structures rather than challenging them.

"And our partnership would be preserved under this arrangement?" I asked.

"Enhanced," Lady Silverleaf said with predatory satisfaction. "Court resources would allow you to explore the full potential of your magical integration without the limitations imposed by academic oversight protocols."

Without the limitations imposed by academic oversight. Which meant without the protection that university independence provided against political manipulation.

"Residence would begin immediately following today's faculty council vote," Lord Darian continued with the casual certainty of someone who considered the outcome predetermined. "Transportation has been arranged."

Through our bond, I felt Ivy's spike of alarm. They weren't just offering relocation, they were announcing it, regardless of what NPU's faculty decided or what we preferred.

"That seems premature," Professor Meridian observed with diplomatic understatement. "The faculty council hasn't voted on custody arrangements."

"The faculty council will vote according to their assessment of what best serves their students' interests," Lady Silverleaf replied smoothly. "But Winter Court authority supersedes academic autonomy when territorial security is involved."

The mask was finally dropping. They'd never intended to honor university independence or student choice. The diplomatic language had been theater designed to make compliance seem voluntary while preparing for forced compliance when voluntary cooperation proved insufficient.

I felt Ivy's architectural consciousness interfacing with NPU's foundational systems in ways that suggested the campus infrastructure was prepared to resist Winter Court authority through means that exceeded simple defensive magic.

But before either of us could respond to their ultimatum, Lord Darian did something that transformed political pressure into personal attack.

He reached into his formal robes and withdrew a scroll sealed with the Blackthorn family crest, not Winter Court authority, but my own inherited legacy.

"Rowan," he said, his voice shifting from diplomatic to familial with calculated intimacy. "There's something else to consider."

The scroll unrolled to reveal a formal document written in the ceremonial script used for court proclamations of highest importance.

"Full reinstatement of Blackthorn family standing," Lord Darian announced with the kind of satisfaction that suggested he'd been saving this for maximum impact. "Restoration of inheritance rights, territorial holdings, and political authority that were suspended following your parents' deaths."

The words hit me like physical blows. Everything I'd lost when the Winter Court had used my parents' accident to justify removing a politically inconvenient family from their traditional positions of authority, offered back in exchange for abandoning the partnership that had given my life meaning.

"Conditional, of course, on your willingness to accept guidance appropriate to your restored position," Lady Silverleaf added with delicate emphasis. "Court training designed to prepare you for the responsibilities that come with territorial authority."

Through our bond, I felt Ivy's understanding of what they were really offering. Not just political restoration, but the promise of power that could protect the people I cared about, if I was willing to sacrifice the person I cared about most.

"And Miss Snowfall?" I asked, my voice steadier than I felt.

"Would be provided with alternative educational arrangements suited to her background and capabilities," the Court Architectural Assessor replied with clinical detachment. "Nothing punitive, naturally. Simply... appropriate to someone without noble heritage."

The phrase scalded. Our binding rune stung my skin, hers first, mine echoing through the connection with sharp heat that spoke to how personally the threat had hit her.

"You want me to choose between my family legacy and my partnership," I said, understanding the full scope of their manipulation.

"We want you to choose between selfish personal attachment and responsible service to the magical community that depends on strong leadership," Lord Darian corrected with moral authority that transformed love into selfishness and abandonment into virtue.

The political beauty of the trap was staggering. They were offering me everything I'd lost, family standing, inherited authority, the power to protect people I cared about, in exchange for proving that I cared more about political position than personal connection.

I felt Ivy's mixture of understanding and terror as she realized they'd found the one offer that might actually tempt me to abandon our partnership. Not because I wanted power for its own sake, but because political authority could protect her from the consequences of defying Winter Court interests.

But I could also feel her architectural consciousness providing insight that transformed the political framework they were trying to impose. The Blackthorn legacy they were offering to restore hadn't been designed to serve Winter Court territorial control, it had been built on collaborative magical development that strengthened the entire northern region rather than concentrating power in the court hierarchy.

"The restored authority would include oversight of magical education throughout the northern territories," Lord Darian continued, clearly recognizing my hesitation as potential acceptance. "You could ensure that institutions like NPU continue to serve their educational mission without interference from political forces that might seek to exploit student capabilities for inappropriate purposes."

The irony was breathtaking. They were offering me the authority to protect NPU from exactly the kind of political manipulation they were currently attempting, provided I demonstrated my reliability by sacrificing the person whose partnership had taught me what collaborative magic could accomplish when it wasn't subordinated to political control.

"Rowan," Ivy said quietly, her voice carrying calm determination that cut through the political complexity with surgical precision. "What do you choose?"

The simple question silenced the entire room. Not asking what I thought about their offer, not seeking analysis of political implications, asking me to declare, publicly and irreversibly, what mattered most.

I looked at Lord Darian's satisfied expression, at Lady Silverleaf's predatory patience, at the Court Architectural Assessor's clinical interest in whether their psychological manipulation would prove sufficient to secure compliance.

Then I looked at Ivy, small, fierce, brilliant Ivy whose architectural inheritance could reshape the foundations of magical education, whose partnership had taught me that some bonds were stronger than political pressure, whose love had shown me that collaborative magic was more powerful than anything territorial authority could offer.

"I choose her," I said with clarity that carried across the crystalline recording devices to whatever analysis committees would review this conversation later. "I choose partnership over position, collaboration over control, love over legacy."

The words resonated through the conference room like spellwork, creating harmonics that made the crystal recording devices hum with sympathetic vibration. Through our bond, I felt Ivy's surge of relief and determination as my choice anchored her own resolve.

"You're choosing to abandon your family's legacy for teenage infatuation," Lady Silverleaf said sharply, her diplomatic composure cracking under the pressure of political strategy that had failed to account for emotional conviction.

"I'm choosing to honor my family's legacy by building something better than what political manipulation destroyed," I replied with certainty that came from understanding the difference between inherited obligation and chosen responsibility.

Lord Darian's expression shifted from satisfied to cold, the familial warmth disappearing behind Winter Court calculation. "This is a mistake, nephew. One that could have consequences extending far beyond your personal preferences."

"Then those consequences are mine to face," I said, reaching for Ivy's hand with a deliberate public gesture that made our partnership unmistakably clear to everyone in the room.

The moment our fingers touched, our binding runes flared with aurora light that had nothing to do with Winter Court activation and everything to do with conscious choice. The light spread outward from our joined hands, creating patterns that interfaced with NPU's foundational systems in ways that made the conference room's crystal surfaces ring with harmonious resonance.

Through our bond, I felt the moment when Ivy's architectural consciousness connected fully with the campus infrastructure, not as inherited privilege but as chosen responsibility. The aurora patterns that filled the room weren't just a magical display, they were protective shields designed to defend educational independence against political authority that sought to transform sanctuary into submission.

"Extraordinary," Professor Blitzen breathed, her electrical magic responding to our display with lightning patterns that reinforced rather than competed with our collaborative casting.

But the Winter Court representatives were less impressed by our magical demonstration than alarmed by its political implications.

"This defiance will be noted," Lord Darian said with the kind of cold authority that preceded consequences designed to make resistance seem foolish in retrospect. "As will your university's complicity in harboring students who refuse legitimate territorial guidance."

"Noted by whom?" Professor Meridian asked with wind sprite authority that suggested she was prepared to defend academic independence against whatever authority they thought they represented.

"By people who understand that magical education serves larger purposes than individual preference," Lady Silverleaf replied with verbal precision that transformed threat into inevitable consequence.

But before they could elaborate on what those consequences might include, the conference room's communication system activated with priority routing that carried aurora patterns I recognized as emergency broadcast protocols.

The message that materialized wasn't Winter Court authority or university administration, it was a campus-wide announcement that pulsed with the kind of urgent energy that meant immediate action was required.

All students and faculty report to the Main Auditorium immediately. Emergency assembly called by the Student Council in coordination with the Faculty Senate. Topic: Preservation of Academic Independence. Student voice will be heard. Time: Now.

From the direction of the Main Auditorium, the lattice beat once, twice, like a drumline waking. Through the crystal windows, we could see banners flashing into being: aurora-ink sigils for independence, frost-clean crests for compliance. The campus was choosing sides, and they wanted to make their choice visible.

"It appears your authority is being questioned by people who have their own opinions about what serves their interests," I said to Lord Darian with satisfaction that came from watching political manipulation meet organized resistance.

The aurora patterns that filled the conference room pulsed brighter, and through the crystal windows, we could see students streaming toward the Main Auditorium with the kind of purposeful energy that suggested they'd been organizing while we'd been enduring political theater.

"The assembly won't change Winter Court authority to act in the interests of territorial security," Lady Silverleaf said with diplomatic language that couldn't quite disguise her alarm at facing organized resistance rather than isolated students.

"But it will demonstrate that some educational institutions are stronger than the political forces that try to control them," Ivy replied with architectural confidence that drew from centuries of magical construction designed to serve collaboration rather than domination.

Through our bond, I felt her certainty that whatever the Winter Court brought to their confrontation with NPU's assembled student body, they'd discover that some partnerships inspired rather than isolated, that some magic built community rather than enforcing hierarchy.

"Together?" she asked.

"Always," I replied, and the word carried the weight of choice made public, defiance declared openly, love defended against every force that tried to use it as leverage for political control.

The aurora patterns that filled Conference Room 1 pulsed once more with warm light that belonged to us rather than any external authority, then began moving toward the Main Auditorium where hundreds of students were gathering to prove that some educational institutions were worth defending.

Whatever the Winter Court tried next, they'd face not just two students who'd chosen each other over political convenience, but an entire campus that had decided academic independence was worth fighting for.

The binding rune on my wrist pulsed with steady light as we followed the aurora patterns toward whatever confrontation awaited us in the Main Auditorium.

Some choices, once made, transformed everything that followed.

Time to discover what kind of future could be built on the foundation of partnerships that refused to be controlled.

CHAPTER TWENTY-ONE

ALL IS LOST

IVY

The Main Auditorium had been transformed into a battlefield disguised as a democratic forum.

Students packed the tiered seating in clusters that made their political allegiances unmistakable, independence supporters wore aurora-ink sigils that pulsed with defiant light, while Winter Court sympathizers displayed frost-clean crests that gleamed with cold authority. The air between the factions shimmered with barely contained magical tension, creating pressure that made my binding rune pulse with warning rhythm.

I felt Rowan's mixture of pride and apprehension as he took in the scope of the student organization that had developed in the hours since our confrontation with the Winter Court delegation. Hundreds of students had chosen sides, transforming what should have been a faculty administrative decision into a campus-wide political declaration.

"Quite a turnout," Professor Meridian said quietly as she took her position with the faculty voting bloc, her wind sprite magic creating pine-scented air currents that carried the tension of approaching storm-weather. "I've never seen students this organized around institutional politics."

"Because institutional politics have never affected them this directly," Marcus Thornfield replied from his position as student liaison, his Ward Guild credentials making him a natural bridge between academic and political concerns. "They understand that whatever happens here sets precedent for how magical education serves political authority versus student autonomy."

On the central platform, Chancellor Northwind had finally emerged from whatever private negotiations had kept her absent during the preliminary discussions. Her expression carried the careful neutrality of someone who'd spent the intervening hours calculating political consequences rather than educational principles.

Lord Darian sat with the Winter Court delegation in positions of honor that emphasized their authority to influence proceedings regardless of university preferences. Lady Silverleaf maintained predatory patience while the Court Architectural Assessor continued her silent counting, her lips moving in calculations that probably had nothing to do with democratic process.

"Faculty council will now vote on Resolution 847," Chancellor Northwind announced, her voice carrying across the auditorium with magically enhanced projection. "Whether to comply with Winter Court requests for custodial transfer of students Rowan Blackthorn and Ivy Snowfall, or maintain university independence regarding student welfare decisions."

Custodial transfer. The euphemism hit both of us through our connection like physical blows. Not supervision or oversight, possession that would separate us beyond any hope of maintaining the magical integration that had become fundamental to our existence.

"Faculty members will cast votes by magical signature," Chancellor Northwind continued. "Results will be displayed publicly to ensure transparency."

The voting crystals that materialized above the central platform began accepting faculty magical signatures with aurora patterns that sorted into two distinct categories, compliance or independence. Through our bond, I felt Rowan's growing tension as the results began to accumulate in patterns that suggested the outcome would be devastatingly close.

Professor Meridian's signature blazed with wind sprite authority in support of independence. Professor Blitzen's electrical magic reinforced the same position with crackling determination. Dylan and Lyra voted together, their partnership magic creating collaborative patterns that emphasized student autonomy over external control.

But Professor Ember's signature flared with the kind of certainty that came from believing compliance served student safety better than dangerous independence. Professor Frostwick from Advanced Applications voted the same way, her ice magic creating patterns that aligned with Winter Court authority structures. Three professors from the Practical Magic Department followed suit, their combined signatures creating a formidable bloc in favor of custodial transfer.

"Current tally," Chancellor Northwind announced as the voting crystals processed faculty magical signatures. "Compliance: twelve votes. Independence: eleven votes. Two abstentions pending."

We were losing by a single vote, with only two faculty members yet to declare their positions, and one of those was Chancellor Northwind herself, whose administrative authority would carry decisive weight regardless of numerical count.

Professor Asterin from Theoretical Magic Studies cast her vote with obvious reluctance, her star magic creating patterns that spoke to difficult choices made for principled reasons. The crystal sorted her signature into the compliance column, making the tally thirteen to eleven.

"Final vote pending," Chancellor Northwind said, her voice carrying the weight of someone who understood that her decision would determine not just our immediate fate, but the future relationship between NPU and Winter Court political authority.

The auditorium fell silent except for the hum of magical tension from hundreds of students whose educational future depended on whether academic independence could withstand political pressure.

Through our bond, I felt Rowan's understanding that Chancellor Northwind's prolonged absence from preliminary discussions had probably been spent negotiating with Winter Court representatives about what NPU would gain or lose based on her vote. Private arrangements that would make public democracy into political theater.

"As Chancellor of North Pole University," she said with formal authority that carried across the crystal recording devices to whatever analysis committees would review this decision later, "I cast my vote in favor of compliance with Winter Court custodial requests."

The words hit the auditorium like physical blows. Students in the independence section erupted with cries of protest and disbelief, while Winter Court supporters maintained respectful silence that spoke to their understanding that this outcome had been predetermined rather than democratically achieved.

"Final tally," Chancellor Northwind announced above the student chaos. "Compliance: fourteen votes. Independence: eleven votes. Resolution 847 passes. Custodial transfer will commence immediately."

The words dropped into the lightning-still silence that comes after the strike, when you realize everything familiar has just been destroyed.

We'd lost. After everything we'd built, everything we'd fought for, we'd lost by a single vote bought with political pressure rather than a principled decision.

His hand found mine, desperate and unshakable, fingers gripping so tight the bones ached. I pressed my forehead against his, our binding runes flaring between us like dying stars. "Don't let go," I whispered, the words barely audible even to him. "Whatever happens, don't let go."

Never, his mental voice carried the weight of broken promises we couldn't keep. *But they're going to try to make us.*

The auditorium blurred, sound tunneling like I'd been plunged under ice. Not the bond, that burned stronger than ever, fed by desperation. But hope. The belief that choosing each other could be enough against forces that commanded centuries of political authority.

"Consent is not required when territorial security is involved," Lady Silverleaf replied with satisfaction that suggested she'd been waiting for exactly this moment of defiance. "Winter Court authority supersedes individual preference when broader magical interests are at stake."

But before anyone could respond to her assertion, something unexpected began happening in the student seating sections.

Marcus Thornfield rose from his position as student liaison, his Ward Guild credentials gleaming with magical authority that rivaled faculty standing. "Student Council calls for formal objection to Resolution 847 on grounds of procedural violation."

"What procedural violation?" Chancellor Northwind asked with sharp attention.

"The resolution addresses custodial transfer of students

without student representation in the voting process," Marcus replied with legal precision that suggested he'd been preparing for exactly this moment. "NPU charter requires student voice in decisions that affect student welfare."

The auditorium erupted with renewed energy as students in the independence section realized that the democratic process might still provide protection against political manipulation. But it wasn't just voices rising, it was magic.

Earth sprites in the front rows stomped their feet in synchronized rhythm, each impact sending vibrations through the auditorium's foundation that awakened dormant protective spells woven into the architecture itself. Fire elementals raised their hands, sparks cascading from their fingertips to form constellation patterns across the vaulted ceiling. Water sprites created halos of condensation that caught the light and reflected it in prismatic displays that spoke to unified resistance rather than individual defiance.

Air magic from a dozen wind sprites created currents that carried the voices of students who'd never spoken publicly before: "Student voice! Student choice! Our campus, not your politics!"

I watched sprites whose magic I'd barely noticed in three years of classes working together to create collaborative spellwork that exceeded anything in our curriculum. Light constructs from my fellow illumination specialists began weaving together into ward frameworks, while frost mages, led by students who'd probably never agreed on anything before, provided structural reinforcement that turned the entire auditorium into a protective magical working.

I felt Rowan's awe matching my own as we realized that our partnership hadn't just inspired political support, it had taught our classmates what collaborative magic could accomplish when it served a chosen community rather than imposed authority.

"Student objections are noted," Lord Darian said with dismissive authority. "But Winter Court territorial jurisdiction supersedes academic procedural requirements when magical security is involved."

"Then you're acknowledging that this isn't about student welfare," I said with architectural consciousness that drew from understanding how educational institutions should serve collaborative development rather than external political control. "It's about territorial control that uses student custody as leverage for broader authority."

The accusation carried across the auditorium with clarity that made the political implications unmistakable. Through our bond, I felt Rowan's admiration for my willingness to challenge them publicly, along with his growing certainty that public defiance would make Winter Court's response more severe rather than less.

"Miss Snowfall," Lady Silverleaf said with dangerous pleasantness, "you seem to be under the impression that individual preference matters more than institutional responsibility."

"I'm under the impression that institutional responsibility includes protecting students from political manipulation disguised as protective custody," I replied with determination that had been building since the moment they'd first tried to separate us.

But even as I spoke, Winter Court enforcement personnel were moving into position around the auditorium's exits. Not the diplomatic representatives who'd been conducting negotiations, armed guards whose magical signatures radiated the kind of authority that ended disagreements through force rather than persuasion.

"Custodial transfer will proceed as scheduled," Lord Darian announced with finality that brooked no further argument. "Mr.

Blackthorn will accompany Winter Court representatives to facilities appropriate to his restored family standing. Miss Snowfall will be relocated to educational arrangements suited to her background and capabilities."

The euphemisms couldn't disguise what they were really announcing, our immediate separation, regardless of magical consequences or personal preferences.

I could feel Rowan's storm magic beginning to spike toward the destructive patterns that characterized the Blackthorn curse under extreme pressure. But instead of the chaotic violence that usually resulted from loss of control, his power reached for mine with desperate precision, seeking the stability that our partnership provided.

I responded instinctively, my light magic flowing toward his frost power with enhanced synchronization that created aurora patterns across the auditorium's crystalline ceiling. Not just magical collaboration, protective defiance that drew from architectural consciousness to reinforce our bond against external attempts to break it.

The binding runes on both our arms flared with brilliant light that had nothing to do with Winter Court activation and everything to do with conscious choice to resist separation. Through our enhanced connection, I felt the moment when our magical signatures locked into integration so complete that forced separation would destroy us both.

"They can't break us apart," Rowan said with certainty that came from understanding our bond had evolved beyond anything Winter Court political science could control. "Whatever they try, whatever force they use, we're stronger together than anything they can bring against us separately."

But even as he spoke, I could see from Lord Darian's satisfied expression that they'd been anticipating exactly this kind of magical resistance. The enforcement personnel weren't just armed guards, they were specialists trained to handle magical partnerships that refused to comply with political authority.

"Magical enforcement is authorized," Lady Silverleaf announced with cold precision. "Resistance will be interpreted as rebellion against territorial security interests."

The temperature dropped ten degrees in a heartbeat. Frost-rime marched down the aisles like advancing soldiers, and the air turned sharp with the ozone bite of charged battle spells.

Magical enforcement. The euphemism for the kind of force that would separate us regardless of magical consequences or personal cost.

Through our bond, I felt Rowan's protective fury building toward levels that would either destroy everything around us or forge our partnership into something unbreakable. His hands found mine with desperate precision, our fingers intertwining as our binding runes synchronized into a rhythm that spoke to shared heartbeat and unified determination.

"Whatever happens," he said quietly, his voice carrying across our mental connection with intimacy that no external authority could touch, "we face it together."

"Together," I agreed, letting my architectural consciousness flow through our bond to anchor his storm magic before it could turn destructive. "Even when they try to pull us apart."

The aurora patterns above us pulsed with protective light that belonged to us rather than any political authority, while around the auditorium, students began chanting with growing intensity: "Our magic, our choice! Our campus, our voice!"

But through the crystalline windows, I could see additional Winter Court enforcement arriving, sleighs filled with specialists whose only purpose was ensuring that political authority prevailed over individual resistance.

The faculty vote had been predetermined. The procedural challenges were being dismissed. The enforcement was moving into position.

And in minutes, they would attempt to tear apart a bond that had become fundamental to our magical existence, regardless of whether we survived the process.

Through our joined hands, I felt Rowan's storm magic settling into calm determination that spoke to shared resolve rather than individual desperation. Whatever the Winter Court brought against us, they'd discover that some partnerships were stronger than the political frameworks designed to control them.

Even if defending that truth cost us everything we'd built together.

The binding rune on my wrist pulsed with steady light as enforcement personnel began moving toward the central platform where we sat, their magical signatures radiating the kind of authority that had ended countless individual resistance efforts throughout Winter Court history.

But as they approached, something unexpected began happening in the student seating sections. The chanting was growing more organized, more unified, building toward something that felt less like protest and more like collaborative magical working.

Aurora patterns were beginning to form above the independence supporters, not random displays of defiant energy, but structured light constructs that looked suspiciously like ward formations. Defensive magic created through collective effort, designed to protect rather than attack.

Hundreds of students were preparing to defend our partnership through collaborative spellwork that drew from everything NPU had taught them about the power of choosing to work together.

The enforcement personnel paused in their approach, clearly recognizing that separating two bound students had become significantly more complicated when those students were surrounded by hundreds of allies willing to use magic to protect them.

"Stand down," Lord Darian commanded with authority that expected immediate compliance. "This is Winter Court business, not a student concern."

"Our classmates' welfare is absolutely our concern," Marcus Thornfield replied with Ward Guild authority that spoke to legal understanding as well as magical capability. "And we're prepared to defend it."

The standoff that followed felt like the moment before lightning strikes, charged air, suppressed energy, the certainty that whatever happened next would change everything about the relationship between educational institutions and political authority.

"If they want to separate us," he said through our mental connection, his thoughts carrying warmth that anchored my own growing determination, "they'll have to go through everyone who believes that some choices should be protected rather than controlled."

Around us, the aurora ward formations continued building, supported by students whose magical education had taught them that collaboration could accomplish things that individual effort never could. What had started as a political protest was transforming into something more powerful, a living demonstration that educational collaboration could challenge political authority when it served principles worth defending.

I felt ice sprites channeling their magic into crystalline supports that reinforced the light constructs other students were creating. Plant manipulators coaxed vines from decorative arrangements to form physical barriers between the enforcement personnel and our position on the central platform. Even students whose magic had always seemed purely academic, theoretical specialists and history researchers, were contributing energy that fed the collaborative working with scholarly precision.

Near the entrance, a timid first-year lifted her note-taking stylus like a wand, her minor illumination magic adding its glow to the growing ward structure. Petal Brightwood tossed her own stylus in a perfect arc that became a light-anchor, pulling other magical threads into stable formation. A senior translator I recognized from Advanced Linguistics wove legal runes into the protective patterns, adding binding force that would make the wards harder to dismiss as mere student theatrics.

The Winter Court had come to NPU expecting to face two isolated students whose resistance could be overcome through superior force.

Instead, they were discovering that some partnerships inspired community rather than creating isolation, that some bonds strengthened educational institutions rather than threatening them.

"If they want to separate us," he said through our mental connection, his thoughts carrying warmth that anchored my own growing determination, "they'll have to go through everyone who believes that some choices should be protected rather than controlled."

Time to find out which was stronger, political authority backed by centuries of territorial control, or educational collaboration supported by people who'd chosen to build something better together.

The binding rune pulsed with light that belonged to us and everyone who'd chosen to stand with us, while overhead the aurora wards continued growing into protective patterns that spoke to the power of chosen partnership defended by chosen community.

All was not lost. Not yet.

The Winter Court enforcement personnel raised their weapons with synchronized precision that spoke to military training rather than diplomatic resolution. Lady Silverleaf's smile widened with predatory satisfaction, as if student resistance had been exactly what she'd been hoping to provoke. Chancellor Northwind stepped forward, her expression calculating the political cost of whatever orders she was about to give.

The auditorium held its breath, magic crackling in the air like the moment before lightning strikes, while hundreds of students prepared to discover whether collaborative spellwork could protect what they'd chosen to defend.

CHAPTER TWENTY-TWO
DARK NIGHT OF THE SOUL

ROWAN

The chaos in the Main Auditorium provided perfect cover for disappearing.

Stun bolts cracked against crystalline barriers as we slipped through a service door. The wards held, long enough for the building to conspire in our escape. The architectural consciousness Ivy had inherited guided us through passages that responded to her presence with welcoming warmth, seals opening at her touch, while corridors led us deeper into NPU's foundations.

"Where are we going?" I asked through our mental connection, not wanting to risk voices carrying through corridors that might still be monitored by Winter Court surveillance spells.

Somewhere they can't follow, she replied, her thoughts carrying determination mixed with something that felt like homecoming. *Somewhere that belongs to us rather than them.*

The passages she led us through descended deeper into NPU's foundations than I'd ever been, past the sub-levels where Dylan and Lyra conducted their research, into architectural strata that predated Winter Court influence entirely. Here, the walls were carved from living ice that held aurora patterns within its crystalline depths, illuminated by magic that drew from sources older than political authority.

This is where it all began. Ivy's mental voice carried wonder as we moved through corridors that recognized her bloodline. *The original collaborative magic that created NPU's foundations. Before anyone thought to use a partnership for territorial control.*

I felt her growing understanding of what her family had built, not just infrastructure, but philosophy made manifest. Educational collaboration designed to serve magical development rather than political objectives, partnership magic that strengthened individuals rather than subsuming them into external authority structures.

The passage we followed opened into a circular chamber I recognized from our shared dreams, the space where partnership magic had been developed as art rather than weapon, collaboration rather than control. The Founders' Chamber, where the first collaborative bonds had been forged not for political advantage but for the joy of building something beautiful together.

Seeing it with waking eyes revealed details that dream-sharing had missed.

Portraits carved into ice didn't show propaganda. They showed people, hands extended, hands accepted, partnerships that chose each other even when it cost everything. Each portrait pulsed with residual emotional resonance, love that had transcended magical compatibility to become something deeper, partnerships that had chosen each other despite forces that tried to tear them apart.

"They all faced this," Ivy said quietly, her voice carrying across the chamber with architectural acoustics that made whispers seem like pronouncements. "The choice between what others wanted them to be and what they chose to become together."

I studied the portraits with a growing understanding of my own of what she meant. Not just magical partnerships, but political resistance disguised as personal choice. People who'd refused to let their collaborative capabilities serve external authority, who'd built something beautiful instead of something useful to others' objectives.

"And they all chose each other," I said, noting the way each portrait showed deliberate gesture, hands extended in offers that had been accepted rather than compelled.

"Even when it cost them everything else they could have had," Ivy agreed, her light magic responding to the chamber's ancient illumination patterns with recognition that went beyond conscious knowledge.

Through our bond, I felt her awareness of what our own choice would cost, not just comfort or safety, but the entire future I'd been raised to expect. Blackthorn authority, Winter Court standing, the political power that could protect people I cared about. All of it conditional on abandoning the person who'd taught me what partnership could accomplish when it wasn't subordinated to political control.

"Are you afraid?" she asked. I could feel the weight of her own fears. Not just of Winter Court authority or magical separation, but of being wrong about what we meant to each other. Of discovering that our bond was a magical compulsion rather than a genuine connection, political convenience rather than chosen love.

"Terrified," I admitted, settling beside her on the crystalline bench that occupied the Founders' Chamber's center. "Not of them. Of waking up one day and realizing what I feel is scaffolding, not stone. Magic, not choice."

The confession hung between us with the weight of honesty I'd never offered anyone else. Through our bond, I felt her surprise at my vulnerability, followed by her understanding that the same fear had been eating at her since the moment people started suggesting our partnership was compulsion rather than choice.

"What if it started as compulsion but became choice?" she asked quietly. "What if the magic brought us together, but what we built from that connection belongs to us?"

Her hand found mine with familiar precision, our binding runes settling into a synchronized rhythm that spoke to shared heartbeat and unified determination. The contact felt consciously chosen rather than magically required.

"Then we decide what we are based on what we want to be," I replied, letting my storm magic flow toward her light power with enhanced synchronization that created aurora patterns across the Founders' Chamber's crystalline surfaces. "Not what anyone else wants to use us for."

The light that bloomed from our joined hands wasn't just a magical collaboration, it was conscious choice made visible, partnership that drew from compatibility but transcended compulsion. Through our bond, I felt the moment when our shared resolve crystallized into something that belonged to us rather than the forces that had shaped it.

"I love you," Ivy said simply, the words carrying across the chamber with architectural acoustics that made them seem like pronouncements rather than whispered confessions. "Not because magic makes me, not because proximity requires it, but because being with you feels like coming home to someone I didn't know I'd been missing."

The declaration hit me with force that had nothing to do with magical binding and everything to do with emotional truth I'd been afraid to acknowledge. Through our connection, I felt her certainty that whatever had brought us together, what we'd become together was worth defending against anyone who tried to reduce it to political convenience.

"I love you too," I replied, the words feeling both inevitable and revolutionary. "I love your courage when you're terrified, your determination to build rather than break, the way you make my magic remember what it was meant to be before anyone turned it into a weapon."

I heard her sharp intake of breath, followed by a feeling of warmth that had nothing to do with magical enhancement and everything to do with being seen completely and loved anyway.

"What do we do now?" she asked, though through our connection I could feel that she already knew the answer.

"We choose each other," I said, rising from the crystalline bench and extending my hand in deliberate echo of the portraits that surrounded us. "Publicly, permanently, regardless of what it costs."

She squeezed my hand, and together we moved toward the chamber's exit, not the passage that had brought us down, but the spiral staircase carved into the far wall that led upward through NPU's foundations toward the surface.

"Where does this go?" I asked as we climbed, though the answer was becoming obvious as aurora light began filtering down from above.

"Observatory rooftop," Ivy replied with certainty that came from architectural knowledge inherited through centuries of magical construction. "The highest point on campus. Where partnership magic was first demonstrated to the outside world."

The staircase we followed was older than NPU's current buildings, carved from ice that held the warmth of ancient magic rather than the chill of court control. Each step upward felt like moving from hidden truth toward public declaration, from private choice toward shared resistance.

The rooftop itself was breathtaking, a crystalline platform that provided panoramic views of NPU's snow-covered campus while offering direct access to the aurora borealis that danced across the arctic sky. But it was the privacy that struck me most powerfully. No surveillance spells, no political observers, no external authority trying to dictate what our partnership should become.

Just us, the aurora, and the choice that would define everything that followed.

"It's beautiful," Ivy breathed, moving to the platform's edge where crystal barriers provided safety without obstructing the view. "I can see the whole campus from here. Everyone we're fighting for."

Through our bond, I felt her awareness of the student ward formations still maintaining protective magic around the Main Auditorium, the faculty who'd voted for our independence, the collaborative resistance that our partnership had inspired. We weren't just choosing each other, we were choosing to lead a movement that challenged how magical education served political authority.

"They'll come for us," I said, settling beside her close enough that our shoulders touched and our binding runes synchronized into a rhythm that spoke to shared determination. "Once they realize we've disappeared, they'll hunt us down with everything they have."

"Let them," Ivy replied with architectural consciousness that drew from understanding how sanctuary was built to last. "We'll meet them as partners, not as victims of their political manipulation."

Above us, the aurora borealis shifted into patterns that looked suspiciously like celebration, not random natural phenomena, but intentional artistry that responded to our presence with approval. Through our bond, I felt Ivy's recognition of the light displays as architectural magic, her family's legacy welcoming the choice we were making.

"Together?" she asked, turning to face me with frost-colored eyes that held depths of determination and love that made my chest tight with emotions I'd never expected to feel.

"Always," I replied, and the word carried weight that went beyond magical binding or political necessity.

Our runes aligned, and something clicked. The storm inside me found edges, corridors, a plan. Her light didn't just brighten, it measured. Choice wasn't a rush; it was a design. We laid the first line together.

Wind combed the aurora into ribbons; frost haloed her hair. When she looked at me, the whole sky felt like a held breath.

Then Ivy rose on her toes and kissed me with tenderness that spoke to conscious choice rather than desperate need, love freely given rather than magically compelled.

The contact was electric in ways that had nothing to do with our binding runes and everything to do with emotional truth, finally finding physical expression. For the first time since our bond began, there was no ache of magical requirement driving us together, just want, pure and simple. The storm inside me found angles now; her blueprints taught my ice to hold a line. Her lips were soft and warm despite the arctic air, her light magic flowing toward mine with synchronization that created aurora displays across the entire northern sky. When we broke apart, the aurora had already rearranged into blueprints, less celebration than instruction.

"Beautiful," I murmured, though I wasn't talking about the light show.

"Perfect," she agreed.

The kiss had been choice made manifest, partnership that transcended magical compulsion to become conscious collaboration. Whatever the Winter Court brought against us now, they'd face unified resistance rather than isolated students they could separate and control.

"We should go back," Ivy said reluctantly, though through our connection I felt her awareness that the standoff in the Main Auditorium couldn't last indefinitely. "They'll need to know we're choosing to fight rather than hide."

"We'll show them together," I agreed, taking her hand as we moved toward the staircase that would lead us back through NPU's foundations toward whatever confrontation awaited us.

But as we prepared to descend, the lights snapped from celebration to signal, urgent pulses. Below, the lattice screamed data: wards under siege, faculty scattered, enforcement sweeping the halls in grids.

Through our bond, I felt Ivy's architectural consciousness interfacing with campus infrastructure in ways that provided information about what was happening at ground level. But worse than the tactical situation was the magical signature I could feel through her inherited connection to the campus lattice, a houndsnow glyph locked on her bloodline, crystalline and patient, nosing along every stone that remembered Lux and Niveus.

"They're not waiting for us to come back," Ivy realized with growing alarm. "They're hunting us."

"Then we meet them on our terms," I replied, storm magic beginning to build in my chest with controlled fury that had nothing to do with the Blackthorn curse and everything to do with protective determination. "As partners who refuse to be separated by people who think love is a political weakness."

The aurora above us pulsed once more with approval, and

through the observatory's crystal barriers, we could see magical signatures moving across NPU's campus with tracking spells designed to locate specific individuals regardless of how well they tried to hide.

Time to discover whether love consciously chosen was stronger than authority that demanded submission.

Time to find out what partnership magic could accomplish when it served resistance rather than compliance.

The binding rune on my wrist pulsed with steady light as we began our descent through foundations that had been built to protect collaborative magic from political control, carrying us toward a confrontation that would determine the future of magical education and the meaning of chosen partnership.

CHAPTER TWENTY-THREE
FACULTY COUNCIL SHOWDOWN

IVY

The houndsnow glyph locked onto us the moment we emerged from the Founders' Chamber into the Observatory's main corridors.

The air sharpened---ice-mint and iron. The crystalline presence had been waiting, patient as winter itself, ready to snap onto my Lux signature the instant we left the ancient protections. Through the campus lattice, I felt Winter Court enforcement teams converging on our position with systematic precision.

They know where we are, I said through our mental connection, feeling the magical net tightening around the Observatory complex.

Then we don't run, Rowan replied, his storm magic settling into the calm determination I'd come to recognize as his battle-ready state. "We go straight to the emergency faculty session. Make our declaration public before they can take us quietly."

Through the campus lattice, I felt the magical signatures of faculty members already gathering in the Administrative Tower's

crisis management chamber---the secure conference space where
Professor Meridian had called an emergency session. If we could
reach them, we'd have witnesses. Protection through publicity.

This way, I guided us through a maintenance shaft that my
family's construction records showed connecting directly to the
Administrative Tower's sub-basement. Not escape---strategic
positioning. The Winter Court could track us, but they'd have to
extract us in front of the entire faculty council.

"Three minutes," I whispered as we navigated the narrow
passage, feeling our binding runes beginning their familiar
warning pulse. Not from separation---we were pressed close
together in the confined space---but from magical stress. The
houndsnow glyph's presence was interfering with our bond's
stability, creating artificial separation anxiety even though we
were touching.

Time for our entrance, Rowan replied through our mental
connection, his storm magic settling into calm determination that
anchored my own growing magical stress.

The emergency faculty session had been convened in the
Administrative Tower's crisis management chamber, not the
public auditorium where formal votes were conducted, but the
secure conference space where life-and-death academic decisions
were made without external pressure. Through my connection to
NPU's infrastructure, I could feel the magical signatures of faculty
members streaming toward the emergency meeting, their
combined authority creating resonance patterns that spoke to
institutional resistance rather than compliance.

But I could also feel Winter Court enforcement closing the net
around our position with systematic precision that left fewer
escape routes with each passing minute.

"Four minutes," Rowan said aloud as we emerged from the
maintenance shaft into the Administrative Tower's foundation

level. His storm magic was already responding to the stress of approaching separation anxiety, frost patterns beginning to form on the corridor walls despite his careful control.

The emergency session was already in progress when we slipped into the crisis management chamber through a service entrance that connected to the building's original construction. Faculty members had arranged themselves in defensive formation around the central discussion area, while Winter Court representatives occupied positions that emphasized their authority to observe and intervene regardless of academic independence.

", cannot allow external enforcement to dictate university policy," Professor Meridian was saying with wind sprite authority that created sharp air currents throughout the chamber. "The custody resolution was procedurally flawed and strategically compromised."

"The resolution was democratically achieved through established faculty voting protocols," Lady Silverleaf replied with diplomatic precision that couldn't quite disguise her satisfaction at watching academic independence crumble under political pressure. "Winter Court authority to ensure student safety supersedes institutional autonomy when territorial security is involved."

"Correction," Professor Meridian volleyed with procedural authority that made the chamber's crystal fixtures ring with resonance. "NPU Charter 3.2.1, student welfare decisions require student voice present. Your resolution is voidable pending remand."

"Student safety," Professor Blitzen added with electrical energy that made the chamber's crystal fixtures spark dangerously. "You mean political convenience disguised as protective custody."

Through our bond, I felt Rowan's mixture of pride and alarm

as he realized that NPU's faculty were mounting serious resistance to Winter Court authority, but also that resistance was being systematically undermined by legal frameworks that privileged territorial control over educational autonomy.

"Ninety seconds," I whispered, feeling the tower's defenses crumbling faster than I'd anticipated.

Let's show them what we've become, Rowan replied through our mental connection, his storm magic settling into calm determination that anchored my own growing stress.

We stepped into the chamber's central area with synchronized movement that immediately drew attention from faculty members and Winter Court representatives alike. Frost unfurled from Rowan's boots as the council turned, and I felt my architectural consciousness interfacing with the chamber's crystalline infrastructure in patterns that spoke to inherited authority choosing educational principles over territorial control.

"Mr. Blackthorn, Miss Snowfall," Chancellor Northwind said with carefully neutral authority, her smile not reaching her eyes, a negotiator who'd already chosen, now hoping the choice still looked principled. "Winter Court representatives have expressed concern for your welfare following your disappearance from the auditorium."

"Our welfare is not Winter Court concern," I replied with architectural consciousness that drew from centuries of magical construction designed to serve educational collaboration rather than political control. "We're NPU students, subject to university authority rather than external territorial claims."

"You're subjects with magical capabilities that affect Winter Court infrastructure throughout the northern region," the Court Architectural Assessor interjected with clinical precision that reduced us to technical problems requiring political solutions.

"Your disappearance represents a security risk that supersedes academic administrative boundaries."

"Security risk," Rowan repeated with winter magic that created frost patterns on the chamber's crystalline surfaces. "Because we refuse to let our partnership serve external political objectives rather than our own educational goals."

"Because your partnership has demonstrated capabilities that require responsible oversight," Lord Darian replied with familial authority that emphasized blood connection over individual autonomy. "Capabilities that could destabilize established magical infrastructure if left uncontrolled."

Uncontrolled. The word hit both of us through our connection like a physical blow. "Uncontrolled to you means 'not yours,'" I said with architectural authority that drew from inherited knowledge. "To us it means not weaponized."

"Two minutes," Rowan said quietly, and through our bond, I felt the storm magic building in his chest as separation anxiety began affecting his ability to maintain careful control. I grounded him with a palm against his sternum, feeling his heartbeat steady under my touch.

But before anyone could respond to the Winter Court's latest ultimatum, something unexpected began happening in the chamber's crystalline infrastructure.

Aurora patterns started forming along the walls, not random displays of magical energy, but structured light constructs that looked suspiciously like the ward formations students had been creating in the Main Auditorium. Through my architectural consciousness, I felt the campus lattice responding to our presence with recognition that went beyond individual bloodline acknowledgment.

The original Lux and Niveus construction protocols were awakening, but they were being overlaid with something new, collaborative magic that combined my inherited knowledge with Rowan's evolving storm control to create protective patterns that served educational independence rather than territorial authority.

"Extraordinary," Professor Meridian breathed, her wind sprite magic responding to the emerging ward formations with supportive air currents that fed the collaborative working. "The infrastructure is defending academic autonomy."

"The infrastructure is responding to bloodline recognition protocols," Lady Silverleaf corrected with sharp attention to the magical signatures interfacing with NPU's foundational systems. "Lux and Niveus heritage commands Winter Court installations regardless of current political arrangements."

"Blood opens doors," I replied with architectural consciousness that drew from centuries of inherited knowledge. "Choice decides what gets built inside."

But even as she spoke, I could feel through my connection to the campus lattice that her interpretation was incomplete. The infrastructure wasn't just responding to inherited authority, it was recognizing conscious choice to use that authority in defense of educational principles rather than political control.

"One minute," I said aloud, feeling our binding runes beginning to flare with warning light as separation anxiety approached dangerous levels.

Through our bond, I felt Rowan's understanding that we needed to make our declaration now, before magical stress compromised our ability to speak with clarity and conviction.

"We choose each other," I said with architectural authority that carried across the chamber's crystalline recording devices to whatever analysis committees would review this confrontation later. "Not because magic compels us, not because political convenience requires it, but because partnership chosen freely is stronger than any bond imposed through external manipulation."

"We choose collaboration over control," Rowan added with storm magic that reinforced the aurora ward formations spreading across the chamber's walls. "Educational development over territorial authority, love over political leverage."

The words resonated through the crisis management chamber with harmonics that made the crystal fixtures ring with sympathetic vibration. Around us, the aurora patterns that had been forming along the walls pulsed brighter, creating protective displays that spoke to the power of conscious partnership defended by institutional infrastructure.

But more than the magical spectacle was the response from faculty members who'd been watching our interaction with growing understanding of what was really at stake.

"Student voice confirmed," Professor Meridian announced with official authority that carried the weight of academic procedure. "Partnership declared voluntary rather than compulsory. University independence maintained."

"Seconded," Professor Blitzen said immediately, her electrical magic reinforcing the ward formations with lightning patterns that made the protective displays stronger rather than competing with them.

Dylan and Lyra exchanged glances from their positions near the chamber's research monitoring station, then stepped forward with partnership magic that created collaborative patterns supporting our declaration.

"Partnership magic research confirms voluntary emotional bonding underlying magical compatibility," Lyra said with academic precision that provided scientific support for our political position.

"Partnership is our method, not your mechanism," Dylan

added with fox-shifter directness that cut through diplomatic language.

Through our bond, I felt Rowan's surprise at how quickly faculty support was crystallizing around our public declaration. Not just individual professors defending academic independence, but institutional resistance organizing around principles that transcended political convenience.

But the Winter Court representatives were less impressed by our faculty support than alarmed by the implications of infrastructure that responded to collaborative magic rather than territorial authority.

"Enough," Lord Darian said with cold precision that silenced the chamber's growing momentum. "Winter Court enforcement authority is activated. Territorial security supersedes academic independence when regional stability is threatened."

"Regional stability," Professor Meridian repeated with wind sprite authority that created sharp air currents throughout the chamber. "Threatened by two students whose magical partner-ship strengthens educational infrastructure rather than chal-lenging it."

"Threatened by magical capabilities that interface with instal-lations throughout Winter Court territory," the Court Architec-tural Assessor replied with clinical detachment that reduced our partnership to technical problem requiring political solution. "Capabilities that require controlled application rather than autonomous development."

As she spoke, I felt a chill that had nothing to do with the chamber's temperature. Through my connection to NPU's infrastructure, I sensed Winter Court enforcement teams moving into position around the Administrative Tower, not diplomatic observers anymore, but military specialists preparing for extrac-tion, regardless of university resistance.

The houndsnow sigil bayed through the stone, soft, relentless, then the tower's wards answered with a bass note I felt in my bones.

"Magical enforcement authorized," Lady Silverleaf announced with satisfaction that suggested student defiance had been exactly what she'd hoped to provoke. "Territorial authority super- sedes academic autonomy when regional security requires direct intervention."

I felt Rowan's storm magic responding to the threat with controlled fury that found architectural angles rather than turning destructive. The aurora ward formations that had been spreading across the chamber's walls pulsed brighter, drawing energy from our synchronized magical signatures to create protective patterns that served educational independence rather than territorial control.

But outside the crisis management chamber, I could feel through the campus lattice that Winter Court enforcement was moving beyond diplomatic pressure to direct action. Not just seeking our voluntary compliance anymore, but preparing to extract us regardless of institutional resistance or personal choice.

"Then they'll discover what academic infrastructure can accomplish when it defends principles rather than serving polit- ical convenience," I said with architectural consciousness that interfaced with NPU's foundational systems in ways that prepared the entire campus for collaborative resistance.

The chamber's crystalline surfaces rang with harmonics that spoke to foundations built to last, partnerships chosen rather than imposed, and the understanding that some educational institutions were worth defending against any authority that tried to reduce them to political tools.

Whatever the Winter Court brought against us next, they'd face not just two students who'd chosen each other, but an entire university whose infrastructure had been designed to protect collaborative magic from forces that sought to control it.

The Administrative Tower's windows went winter-black as sleigh shadows eclipsed the aurora. A hundred enforcement sigils lit in unison, a net tightening. "Doors," Rowan breathed.

The lattice answered: Not today.

From the quad, a roar, students' ward-song rising, threaded with Meridian's wind and Blitzen's lightning. NPU wasn't hiding its pulse anymore. It was marching to the front.

We weren't facing this alone anymore.

The entire campus was choosing sides, and the battle for the future of magical education was about to begin.

CHAPTER TWENTY-FOUR
DEFIANCE

ROWAN

The Winter Court attack came at dawn, precise and overwhelming.

Not the diplomatic pressure or political maneuvering that had characterized their previous attempts to secure our compliance, direct magical assault designed to extract us from NPU regardless of institutional resistance or personal choice. Through the Administrative Tower's crystal barriers, I watched enforcement sleighs descend in formation patterns that spoke to military coordination rather than academic intervention.

Seventy-three enforcement specialists, Ivy's mental voice carried architectural consciousness interfacing with campus surveillance systems. *Plus siege equipment designed to break through educational wards.*

We'd spent the night in the crisis management chamber, maintaining physical contact to satisfy the binding's proximity requirements while faculty members organized resistance around us. Professor Meridian had coordinated with Dylan and Lyra to create layered defensive magic that drew from NPU's foundational systems, while Professor Blitzen had electrified the tower's outer barriers with lightning patterns designed to discourage direct assault.

But as Winter Court enforcers began their systematic approach to the Administrative Tower, it became clear that academic defensive magic, however sophisticated, hadn't been designed to withstand the kind of territorial authority they brought to bear.

"Structural integrity compromised on levels one through three," Professor Meridian reported with wind sprite precision, alarm showing anyway. "Their siege spells are designed specifically to counter educational ward formations."

The air tasted of ozone and burnt crystal. Through our bond, I felt Ivy's architectural consciousness interfacing with NPU's infrastructure in ways that provided real-time analysis of the damage Winter Court enforcement was inflicting. Not just physical assault on the tower's crystalline barriers, but systematic dismantling of magical protections that had defended the university for centuries.

They're not trying to capture us quickly, she realized with growing horror. *They're demonstrating that NPU can't protect anyone who defies Winter Court authority.*

"Evacuation protocols activated for non-essential personnel," Chancellor Northwind announced, watching them assault her university stripping away whatever private arrangements she'd made with Winter Court representatives. Whatever political calculations had driven her compliance vote, seeing a direct attack on educational autonomy had apparently clarified where her loyalties ultimately lay.

But even as faculty members and administrative staff began to organize a withdrawal from the tower's lower levels, something else was happening across NPU's campus that spoke to resistance rather than retreat.

Student magical signatures were organizing into collaborative formations that drew from everything our partnership had taught them about the power of choosing to work together. Not random defensive magic, but structured ward networks that interfaced with NPU's foundational systems to create protective patterns that exceeded anything in current academic theory.

"Marcus is coordinating student response from the Main Auditorium," Dylan reported from his position near the chamber's communication station. "They're using partnership techniques to amplify individual casting capabilities."

I could feel Ivy's mixture of pride and terror as she realized that our relationship had inspired campus-wide magical innovation. Students who'd never worked together before were discovering what collaborative consciousness could accomplish when it served chosen community rather than imposed authority.

"Fourth level breached," Professor Blitzen announced with electrical tension that made the chamber's crystalline surfaces spark dangerously. Static lifted my hair; ice dust bit our lungs as the tower's outer defenses collapsed. "They'll reach the crisis management level within minutes."

The proximity clock didn't stop when we began to move; it changed, now it ticked for the whole campus.

Time to stop hiding, I said through our mental connection, feeling storm magic building in my chest with controlled fury that had nothing to do with the Blackthorn curse and everything to do with protecting the person and institution I'd chosen to defend.

We rose from our defensive positions behind the chamber's reinforced barriers and moved toward the central area where crystalline walls provided clear sightlines to the Winter Court enforcement teams ascending through the tower's compromised levels. Not fleeing or hiding from confrontation, but choosing to meet territorial assault with shared mind that served educational principles rather than political control.

The moment we stepped into the chamber's central space, our binding runes flared with brilliant light that had nothing to do with proximity requirements and everything to do with conscious choice to defend what we'd built together. Through our enhanced connection, I felt the moment when our magical signatures synchronized beyond anything we'd achieved before, not just compatibility or collaboration, but a conscious merger that created something fundamentally new.

The shared consciousness that manifested wasn't just enhanced magical capability, it was visible unity that made our combined thoughts appear as aurora patterns across the chamber's crystalline surfaces. Through crystalline walls, through barriers, through every transparent surface in the Administrative Tower, anyone could see the geometric formations that represented our mental connection made manifest.

Two voices speaking as one appeared in flowing script across the chamber's walls as our thoughts became visible to everyone watching. *Two magical cores united by choice rather than compulsion.*

"Extraordinary," Professor Meridian breathed, her wind sprite magic responding to our display with supportive air currents that fed the collaborative working. "Shared consciousness made visible."

But it wasn't just the spectacle that made faculty members and Winter Court enforcers pause in their respective preparations, it was the power. Storm magic and architectural light flowing together with perfect synchronization to create defensive patterns that drew from centuries of magical development, enhanced by emotional truth that had been consciously chosen rather than magically imposed.

The first Winter Court enforcement team reached the crisis management level with weapons raised and extraction spells prepared for immediate deployment. But the moment they attempted to breach the chamber's defensive barriers, they encountered resistance that exceeded anything in their tactical planning.

Not just individual ward formations or academic protective magic, but the merger turning defensive spellwork into architectural art. My storm magic found angles and corridors that Ivy's inherited knowledge could direct, while her light constructs provided structural frameworks that gave my frost power applications that transcended simple destruction.

"Warning: cease magical resistance or face escalated enforcement action," the lead enforcer announced with authority that expected immediate compliance.

"Counter-warning," Ivy replied with architectural consciousness that drew from centuries of educational magic designed to serve collaboration rather than control. "Cease assault on educational institution or face consequences you're not prepared for."

The exchange might have continued as verbal sparring, but through our enhanced connection, I felt Ivy's growing awareness of what was happening across NPU's campus. Not just student resistance in isolated pockets, but campus-wide magical working that drew from our collaborative consciousness to create protective patterns that encompassed the entire university.

They're linking to us, she realized with awe and alarm. *The students, the faculty who chose resistance, they're using our consciousness as a template for their own collaborative magic.*

Through our bond, I felt the moment when our individual partnership became the foundation for community-wide resistance. Not just two people choosing each other, but an entire educational institution choosing collaboration over control, partnership over domination, conscious connection over imposed authority.

The aurora patterns that had been displaying our shared thoughts across the chamber's surfaces suddenly exploded outward, racing through NPU's crystalline infrastructure to appear on every transparent surface throughout the campus. Windows, barriers, decorative crystals, all of them showing the geometric formations that represented collaborative consciousness choosing to defend educational principles against territorial authority.

"Campus-wide diffusion confirmed," the Court Architectural Assessor reported, her knuckles tapping crystal in rapid calculation as she witnessed magical development that exceeded Winter Court theoretical understanding. "Recommend immediate tactical escalation to prevent cascade spread."

Cascade. The word hit both of us through our connection with the weight of Winter Court fear. They weren't just trying to capture two students whose resistance had become inconvenient, they were trying to prevent the spread of magical innovation that could challenge the foundation of territorial control throughout the northern region.

"Escalated enforcement authorized," Lord Darian announced with cold precision that silenced the chamber's growing magical momentum. "Territorial security supersedes individual welfare when regional stability is threatened."

The tactical shift was immediate and devastating. Winter Court enforcers stopped attempting surgical extraction and began deploying siege magic built to crush the merger by brute force.

But they had miscalculated what our partnership had become.

The first banishment seam whined through the tower, the kind of sound you feel in your fillings. Our shield web quavered, a hairline crack spidering through the chamber's primary barrier. Ice shards cut my cheek; Ivy's light thinned to thread-fine strands.

Then the campus found us. A hundred small partnerships clicked in, one after another, like stars deciding to be a constellation. The seam buckled. Their spell didn't break us; it fed us.

Not just resistance or deflection, but transformation. The severance magic that should have shattered our shared consciousness instead fed it, providing energy that our merged magical cores converted into something beautiful rather than destructive.

Perfect synchronization appeared in flowing aurora script across every surface in the Administrative Tower as our collaborative consciousness reached levels that exceeded individual magical identity. *Two hearts, one rhythm. Two minds, shared purpose. Two magical cores, unified choice.*

For a heartbeat that lasted eternity, we weren't Rowan and Ivy anymore, we were something new, something that belonged to us rather than the forces that had tried to shape it. His thumb found my pulse through our shared consciousness; my breath caught in lungs we somehow shared. Shared thoughts, shared magic, shared determination to protect the educational sanctuary that had allowed our partnership to flourish.

The enforcers' weapons passed through us like we were made of aurora light, their extraction spells finding nothing solid to grasp. Through our unified consciousness, we felt their growing panic as they realized that traditional Winter Court tactics were useless against magical development that transcended their understanding of how partnership magic functioned.

"Impossible," Lady Silverleaf breathed, her diplomatic composure cracking under the pressure of witnessing innovation that challenged everything Winter Court authority rested on.

"Not impossible," we replied in perfect unison, our voices

harmonizing in ways that made the chamber's crystalline surfaces ring with sympathetic vibration. "Inevitable."

But even as our collaborative consciousness repelled Winter Court assault, I felt the cost of what we were achieving. Not physical exhaustion or magical depletion, but the growing awareness that we were changing in ways that couldn't be reversed. The merger that had begun as a defensive necessity was becoming a permanent transformation, creating something beautiful but fundamentally different from what either of us had been individually.

We weren't just partners anymore, we were becoming something new, something that belonged to us rather than anyone trying to control it, but something that meant leaving behind the individual identities we'd been before our binding began.

Are you afraid?

Terrified, I replied with honesty that came from sharing not just thoughts but fundamental emotional truth. *And grateful. This is what we choose to become.*

The moment of perfect unity stretched between us like eternity contained in a heartbeat, then began to shift as Winter Court enforcement responded to their tactical failure with something that felt like desperation rather than strategy.

"Dimensional severance protocols authorized," Lord Darian announced with authority that spoke to consequences more severe than simple magical enforcement. "If the merger cannot be contained, it will be isolated."

Dimensional severance. Through our shared understanding, we both recognized the threat they were preparing to deploy. Not capture or extraction, but removal from normal magical reality entirely, banishment to dimensional space where our shared consciousness couldn't interface with NPU's infrastructure or inspire further resistance.

"No," Chancellor Northwind said with authority that surprised everyone in the chamber. "I withdraw Winter Court permission to operate on university grounds. You've escalated beyond diplomatic intervention to assault on educational autonomy."

"University permission is no longer relevant," Lady Silverleaf replied with cold precision. "Territorial authority supersedes academic autonomy when regional security requires direct action."

But even as they prepared dimensional severance magic that would isolate us from everything we'd chosen to defend, something else was happening throughout NPU that spoke to collaborative consciousness extending far beyond our individual partnership.

Through every transparent surface on campus, aurora patterns showed the thoughts and intentions of hundreds of students who'd chosen to link their magical development to our collaborative model. Not just supporting our resistance, but creating their own partnerships that drew from everything our relationship had demonstrated about the power of conscious choice over imposed authority.

Marcus and Frost appeared in flowing script across the Administrative Tower's crystalline barriers as student partnerships manifested their own collaborative consciousness. *Petal and her roommate. Dylan and Lyra extending their research into a practical application.*

"Campus-wide adoption confirmed," Professor Meridian reported with wind sprite authority that carried exhilaration rather than alarm. "Educational partnership magic spreading through voluntary adoption rather than magical compulsion."

Through our unified consciousness, we felt the moment when NPU's student body chose collaboration over isolation, partnership over individual achievement, conscious connection over academic competition. Not because our binding had imposed shared consciousness on them, but because our partnership had shown them what magical education could accomplish when it served a chosen community rather than external authority.

"Containment failed," the Court Architectural Assessor announced, her knuckles tapping crystal in rapid calculation as she processed tactical analysis rather than emotional response. "The merger has achieved institutional propagation."

The Winter Court had spent centuries preventing exactly this kind of magical development, partnership magic that strengthened individuals rather than making them dependent on external authority, collaborative consciousness that created community rather than serving territorial control.

And now an entire university was choosing to adopt magical innovation that could fundamentally challenge how magical education served political objectives throughout the northern region.

"Dimensional severance deployment imminent," Lord Darian announced with cold finality. "If collaborative consciousness cannot be contained, all manifestations will be isolated from standard magical reality."

Not just us anymore, every student partnership that had chosen to link their magical development to collaborative principles we'd demonstrated. Hundreds of students whose only crime was discovering what their magic could accomplish when it served a chosen connection rather than imposed isolation.

We have to choose. Ivy's thoughts flowed through our unified consciousness with clarity that came from an architectural understanding of what dimensional severance would mean. *Accept exile to protect everyone else, or resist and risk everyone.*

Through our shared awareness, I felt her willingness to sacrifice our partnership to protect the community that had chosen to support us. The kind of selfless determination that had made me fall in love with her in the first place, now offered as the ultimate expression of the collaborative consciousness we'd built together.

No, I replied with storm magic that found new applications through architectural consciousness. *We have a third option.*

Instead of accepting isolation or sacrificing community, we chose to transform what Winter Court authority could control. Our collaborative consciousness had drawn from NPU's foundational systems to create something new, not just individual partnership, but institutional innovation that belonged to the university rather than external political forces.

"University autonomy confirmed through collaborative consensus," we announced in perfect unison, our voices carrying across campus through every transparent surface that displayed aurora patterns representing community choice. "Educational institution chooses independence through partnership rather than submission through isolation."

The declaration resonated through NPU's crystalline infrastructure with harmonics that spoke to foundations built to last, partnerships chosen rather than imposed, and the understanding that some educational institutions were worth defending against any authority that tried to reduce them to political tools.

But victory came with a cost that made itself immediately apparent.

"Faculty split confirmed," Professor Meridian reported with wind sprite precision that couldn't mask her growing alarm at institutional consequences of our resistance. "Approximately forty percent supporting Winter Court authority, sixty percent supporting university independence."

NPU itself was fracturing under the pressure of choosing

between territorial authority and educational autonomy. Faculty members who'd spent decades working together were discovering that fundamental disagreements about magical education's purpose couldn't be bridged through diplomatic compromise.

"I stand with Winter Court interests," Professor Ember announced with certainty that had characterized her position throughout the crisis. "Responsible magical education requires external oversight rather than dangerous autonomy."

"I stand with university independence," Professor Blitzen replied with electrical energy that made the chamber's crystalline surfaces spark with contained lightning. "Educational institutions serve student development rather than political convenience."

Through our shared consciousness, we felt the institutional fracture spreading beyond individual disagreements to fundamental questions about what magical education should accomplish and who should control its direction. Our resistance had inspired community-wide collaboration, but it had also forced choices that revealed irreconcilable differences about educational philosophy.

"Renegade status confirmed," Lady Silverleaf announced with satisfaction that spoke to achieving political objectives through different means than originally planned. "Mr. Blackthorn and Miss Snowfall declared enemies of territorial stability, subject to permanent exile from the Winter Court sphere of influence."

Renegades. The label that meant we could never return to normal academic life, never pursue careers that required Winter Court approval, never live anywhere in the northern territories without facing constant threat of renewed enforcement action.

Worth it? she asked through our shared awareness.

Completely, I replied with storm magic that had found its true purpose through architectural consciousness. *This is what we were meant to build together.*

The collaborative consciousness that had begun as a defensive necessity settled into something that felt like home, not just magical compatibility or emotional connection, but a chosen partnership that belonged to us rather than the forces that had tried to shape it.

Around us, NPU continued fracturing under the pressure of institutional choice, but through every transparent surface on campus, aurora patterns showed the collaborative consciousness that hundreds of students had chosen to adopt based on our example.

We'd lost our place in normal magical society, but we'd gained something more valuable, a community that understood what partnership could accomplish when it served a chosen connection rather than external authority.

The Winter Court could declare us renegades, but they couldn't undo the educational innovation we'd sparked or the institutional independence we'd helped NPU achieve.

Some partnerships were worth defending, regardless of cost.

Some love was worth choosing, even when choosing meant exile.

The binding rune on my wrist pulsed with steady light as our shared consciousness settled into patterns that belonged to us rather than anyone trying to control them, while across campus, hundreds of students discovered what their magic could accomplish when it served a partnership they'd chosen for themselves.

Far to the south, Frostbane's beacon pylons answered the aurora patterns, once, twice, then went dark.

CHAPTER TWENTY-FIVE
RENEGADES

IVY

The silence after magical warfare felt like the world holding its breath.

Snow drifted through shattered crystal barriers where Winter Court siege spells had broken NPU's outer defenses. Damaged sigils flickered and died along the Administrative Tower's walls, their aurora patterns fading to ember-glow before disappearing entirely. The air tasted of ozone and spent magic, metallic on the tongue in a way that made my teeth ache.

I tried to step away from Rowan and stumbled as my depth perception wavered, his eyes were still seeing through mine, creating double vision that made the snow-covered courtyard below shift like a kaleidoscope. Through our bond, I felt his matching disorientation as our consciousness separated back into individual awareness after hours of shared merger.

"Dizzy," he said, his voice echoing strangely in my head even though he'd spoken aloud.

"Synesthesia," I replied, tasting winter mint when he flexed his fingers. "How long before we're properly separate again?"

"Dylan estimated twelve to eighteen hours for full cognitive disentanglement," Lyra said, approaching with the careful gait of someone whose magical core had been stretched beyond normal limits. "The after-effects should fade gradually."

Through the broken barriers of the Administrative Tower, I could see students moving across the campus grounds in small groups, tending to classmates who'd overextended themselves during the collaborative casting.

A banner hung from the Observatory's crystal dome, **Our Campus, Our Choice,** though siege magic had torn it nearly in half, leaving only "Our Campus" clearly visible.

Marcus Thornfield emerged from the tower's lower levels with a scroll that bore official university seals. His Ward Guild credentials had apparently qualified him to serve as emergency legal coordinator, documenting the aftermath of NPU's first armed resistance to external authority.

"Casualty report," he announced with grim satisfaction. "Seventeen students treated for magical exhaustion. Three faculty members were hospitalized for overextension during defensive casting. Zero fatalities." He paused, scanning the gathered faces with something that might have been pride. "The collaborative ward networks held."

Zero fatalities. Through our still-connected consciousness, I felt Rowan's relief matching my own. We'd inspired campus-wide magical innovation, but we hadn't led anyone to death or permanent injury.

Looking at those words, I felt an echo of our rooftop promise: *together, always.* We'd kept that vow, even when it meant making enemies of the most powerful magical authority in the northern territories.

"What about the Winter Court forces?" Professor Meridian asked, her wind sprite magic creating air currents that cleared some of the ozone-sharp atmosphere.

"Withdrawn beyond university boundaries," Marcus replied. "But maintaining siege positions. They're not giving up, they're regrouping."

Before anyone could respond to that ominous assessment, Chancellor Northwind's voice echoed across the campus through magically enhanced announcement crystals positioned on every major building.

"Attention NPU community. As of this morning, North Pole University declares provisional independence from Winter Court territorial authority." Her voice carried none of the political calculation that had characterized her earlier decisions. She'd voted for compliance less than forty-eight hours ago, but watching enforcement teams assault her university had apparently clarified that some accommodations weren't worth making. "We will operate under an emergency academic charter until permanent governance structures can be established."

Provisional independence. The phrase should have felt like victory. Instead, through our shared awareness, I felt the weight of what that declaration would cost, not just institutional autonomy, but permanent fracture of the academic community that had been NPU's greatest strength.

"The faculty split is official," Dylan said quietly, consulting readings on a crystalline tablet that showed magical signatures throughout the campus. "Chancellor Northwind's announcement triggered immediate departures. Approximately forty percent of faculty have submitted resignation letters effective immediately."

"Where are they going?" I asked, though I suspected I already knew the answer.

"Winter Court Administrative Academy," Lyra replied with

academic precision that couldn't mask her disappointment. "Professor Ember is organizing a 'Continuity Council' that will maintain traditional magical education standards under court oversight."

Traditional magical education standards. The euphemism for instruction that served political authority rather than student development, partnership magic that strengthened territorial control rather than individual collaboration.

Through our bond, I felt Rowan's mixture of sadness and determination as he realized that our resistance had created exactly the kind of institutional schism that the Winter Court had probably been hoping to provoke. Not direct control over NPU, but fragmentation that weakened educational independence while creating alternative institutions that served their objectives.

Students were already beginning to choose sides. I could see them through the tower's broken barriers, small groups gathered around different faculty members, magical signatures organizing around professors who'd declared loyalty to either university independence or Winter Court authority. Friendships that had lasted years were fracturing along political lines that hadn't existed a week ago.

"Neutral students have until tomorrow evening to declare dormitory and mentor preferences," Marcus continued, reading from documentation that spoke to administrative preparation for institutional division. "Housing assignments will be reorganized accordingly."

"They're splitting the campus," I realized with growing alarm. "Not just faculty, but students. NPU won't survive that kind of division."

"NPU will survive by serving students who choose collaborative education over political indoctrination," Professor Meridian said with wind sprite authority that created subtle air currents carrying the scent of winter forests. "Quality education doesn't require institutional size, it requires institutional commitment to principles worth defending."

But even as she spoke, I could feel through my architectural consciousness that the campus infrastructure was responding to the political division with instability that went beyond simple magical disruption. The foundational systems that my family had built to serve educational collaboration were straining under the pressure of community fracture, creating resonance patterns that spoke to stress rather than harmony.

Renegade. The word hollowed my chest; I thought of my parents' faces if they heard it, of neighbors who'd watched me grow up, learning I'd become an enemy of the state. Not just political disagreement or academic resistance, criminal status that meant I'd lost my place in normal magical society. No going home to visit family, no career prospects that required Winter Court approval, no safe harbor anywhere in the northern territories.

We'd become people without a country, magical practitioners without institutional protection, students who could never again walk into a classroom without checking for exits first.

"Are you sure this is worth it?" Marcus asked quietly, his expression carrying the weight of someone watching friends choose exile for principles that might not survive political reality. "There are other ways to support educational independence that don't require permanent sacrifice."

I looked at the torn banner reading "Our Campus," at the students tending wounded classmates, at the faculty who'd chosen uncertain independence over comfortable compliance. Through our bond, I felt Rowan's certainty matching my own.

"Some things are worth defending regardless of personal cost," I said with architectural consciousness that drew from inherited understanding of what my family had been trying to protect for eighteen years. "Educational collaboration. Chosen partnership. The right to build something beautiful instead of something useful to other people's objectives."

"Worth being outlaws for," Rowan added with storm magic that created gentle frost patterns on the tower's broken barriers.

"Worth everything," I replied, feeling the weight of that truth settle between us with finality that spoke to conscious choice rather than romantic impulse.

Through our shared consciousness, I felt his understanding that we'd just committed to something larger than personal happiness, we'd chosen to become what educational resistance needed, regardless of cost.

"Can't leave campus safely," he said quietly, and through our bond, I felt his calculation of how many NPU students might be tempted by the kind of rewards the Winter Court was offering.

"Shielded zone protocols are available," Dylan offered with fox-shifter practicality that suggested he'd been anticipating this development. "The Observatory complex has defensive capabilities that could maintain sanctuary indefinitely."

"Indefinitely meaning until Winter Court patience runs out and they decide to escalate beyond siege tactics," Lyra added with academic honesty that cut through optimistic planning.

I felt a hand on my shoulder and turned to see Professor Meridian with an expression that carried the weight of difficult decisions made for principled reasons.

"There's another option," she said quietly. "One that serves NPU's long-term interests but requires personal sacrifice from both of you."

Through our bond, I felt Rowan's immediate wariness. Offers that required personal sacrifice from people with bounties on their heads rarely served those people's interests, regardless of how they were framed.

"Temporary exile," Professor Meridian continued. "Leave campus until the political situation stabilizes, allowing NPU to demonstrate institutional independence without the complication of harboring wanted fugitives."

Temporary exile. The phrase hit both of us with the weight of abandonment disguised as strategy. Leave the university we'd helped defend, the community that had chosen to support us, the educational sanctuary that had allowed our partnership to flourish, all to protect it from consequences that our presence might bring.

"How temporary?" Rowan asked with storm magic that created frost patterns on the tower's broken barriers.

"Until Winter Court authority finds other priorities," Professor Meridian replied diplomatically. "Or until political circumstances change sufficiently to allow your safe return."

"Years, then," I said with architectural consciousness that provided understanding of how slowly political circumstances changed when territorial authority was involved. "Maybe decades."

Through our shared awareness, I felt Rowan's mixture of protective determination and bitter acceptance. We could stay and fight, risking the safety of everyone who'd chosen to support us. Or we could leave, protecting the community at the cost of everything we'd built together.

Before either of us could respond to Professor Meridian's proposal, something shifted in the air that made my architectural consciousness prickle with recognition. Not aurora magic this time, but older communication protocols, the kind my parents had taught me as childhood games, never explaining they were actually emergency contact methods.

A whisper that felt like memory: *Solstice Concordance compro-*

mised. Counter-concordance detected. Trust no official channels. Come home.

The voice was my mother's, speaking through inherited magic that bypassed normal surveillance completely. Through our bond, I felt Rowan's understanding that we'd just received family intelligence that went far beyond simple parental concern.

"Your parents?" Rowan asked through our mental connection, and I felt his mixture of protectiveness and strategic calculation as he realized we were being offered answers to questions that had shaped our entire partnership.

Before I could fully process the implications of familial contact, the aurora patterns above NPU's courtyard shifted into emergency distress signals that made my blood run cold with their urgency.

Frostbane compromised, appeared in flowing script across the Administrative Tower's remaining barriers. *Magnus Ironwood and Phoenix Emberwing missing. Need... architects. Coordinates follow.*

Frostbane Academy. Through our bond, I felt Rowan's sharp attention as he recognized the name of NPU's sister institution, another university that operated under Winter Court charter, serving students throughout the southern territories.

"Frostbane's our sister academy," Dylan explained with growing alarm. "If they're sending emergency signals using pre-institutional magic, something catastrophic has happened."

The coordinates that followed the distress message appeared as three-dimensional aurora formations that burned themselves into my architectural consciousness with the precision of inherited knowledge. Not just geographical location, but magical vectors that would allow travel through foundational systems rather than normal transportation networks.

Through our bond, I felt the moment when our individual choice became something larger, not just personal exile or family reunion, but acceptance of responsibility for defending educational principles wherever they were threatened.

"Multiple crises," I said quietly, feeling the pull of three different responsibilities tugging at our shared consciousness. "Frostbane needs immediate help. My parents offer strategic information. NPU needs proof that independence was worth the cost."

"Multiple opportunities," Rowan corrected through our mental connection, his storm magic finding patterns in the chaos that spoke to strategic thinking rather than overwhelming pressure. "We're not choosing one over the others, we're choosing the order we address them."

I felt his hand find mine, solid and warm despite the winter air that carried the scent of snow and spent magic. Through our bond, I felt his certainty that whatever we chose to do next, we'd choose it as partners who'd proven that collaboration could challenge any authority that tried to control it.

"Together?" I asked, echoing the question that had sustained our relationship through every challenge we'd faced, but now the word carried weight that extended far beyond our individual partnership. Together as partners, as representatives of educational independence, as people who'd chosen to defend principles worth preserving.

"Always," he replied.

Chancellor Northwind approached with official documentation that bore NPU's emergency charter seals. "Provisional diplomatic credentials," she said, offering scroll-cases that would provide some protection during travel between educational institutions. "NPU recognizes your authority to act on behalf of academic independence when institutional cooperation is required."

Diplomatic credentials. Not just permission to leave, but official designation as representatives of educational principles worth defending. The kind of authority that could provide protection during travel while making our mission clear to anyone who questioned our presence.

"Marcus is organizing legal appeals," Dylan added with fox-shifter optimism that suggested he believed political solutions might still be possible. "If Winter Court authority can be challenged through proper channels, renegade status could be overturned."

"And if legal appeals fail?" I asked.

"Then educational institutions will need people who understand that some principles are worth defending regardless of personal cost," Professor Meridian replied with wind sprite authority that created air currents carrying the scent of distant forests and open horizons.

I felt the moment when our resolve crystallized into something that had nothing to do with exile and everything to do with choosing purpose that served collaboration rather than political convenience. We weren't being forced to leave NPU, we were choosing to become what educational resistance needed us to be.

I looked around at the students moving slowly across the courtyard, their movements carrying the exhaustion that came from magical overextension and emotional trauma. They'd chosen to fight for us, and now they'd face the consequences of a fractured community and uncertain futures. Through our bond, I felt Rowan's matching thought: *We just finished one war, and three more are calling.*

"When do we leave?" Rowan asked, and through our bond, I felt his understanding that we were accepting more than travel to Frostbane Academy, we were accepting responsibility for defending educational independence wherever it was threatened.

"Tomorrow morning," Chancellor Northwind replied. "Travel arrangements have been coordinated with institutions that support academic cooperation. You won't be traveling entirely alone."

But as we prepared to finalize departure arrangements, the aurora patterns above NPU shifted one final time into configurations that made my architectural consciousness recognize familial magic I hadn't felt since childhood.

Lux and Niveus emergency protocols activated, appeared in a script that looked like my parents' handwriting. *Solstice Concordance compromised. Counter-concordance detected. Trust no official channels. Coordinates encrypted in childhood memories. Come home.*

Come home. The phrase hit me with the weight of family secrets that had been hidden for eighteen years, architectural knowledge that went beyond inherited ability to include active resistance against political forces that sought to control magical education.

Through our bond, I felt Rowan's understanding that we weren't just choosing between NPU and Frostbane Academy, we were choosing between immediate crisis response and long-term strategic planning that could reshape how magical education related to territorial authority throughout the northern region.

"Multiple options," I said quietly, feeling the pull of parental summons that promised answers to questions I'd been asking since our binding began.

"Multiple responsibilities," Rowan agreed through our mental connection. "Frostbane needs immediate help. Your parents offer strategic information. NPU needs proof that educational independence can survive political pressure."

Above us, the aurora patterns continued displaying emergency signals from multiple sources, institutional distress, family communication, political resistance networks that operated beyond Winter Court surveillance. We'd become symbols of educational independence, but symbols that carried responsibility for protecting principles that extended far beyond our individual partnership.

We'd just saved our home by making ourselves outlaws. South, a school, went dark. North, family secrets waited. He squeezed my hand through winter-touched air that tasted of adventure and responsibility in equal measure.

"Road trip?" I said, feeling aurora patterns write navigation coordinates across the sky like a map designed for travelers who'd chosen purpose over safety.

"Let's go," he answered, and the aurora wrote us a constellation of possibilities that belonged to us rather than anyone trying to dictate our choices.

Some partnerships created their own destiny.

Some love was strong enough to defend entire institutions.

The binding rune on my wrist pulsed with steady light as we prepared to discover what collaborative magic could accomplish when it chose to serve educational resistance rather than political control, while behind us, NPU began the difficult work of proving that academic independence was worth whatever it cost to defend.

The End.

Did you enjoy *Junior Jinx*?

Please consider leaving a review on Goodreads, Bookbub, or your favorite retailer. Reviews help me reach new readers.

Read **Senior Spark** the next book in the **North Pole University** series.

Join my Newsletter for weekly writing updates, exclusive content, new releases, sales, and promotions.

ABOUT THE AUTHOR

Positive, uplifting books and stories.

Marie-Hélène Lebeault is the author of *The Evers Series, Clarity Castle, What Happens Next? Readers Decide Which Story Becomes a Book, the Blood Magick Trilogy, Holiday Shifters, Ghost Stories, Defenders of the Realm, Utopia, Chronicles of the Starborne Cadets, Legends Reborn*, as well as a series of picture books called *Fairy Grandmother*. She lives in Canada with her grown children.

www.mhlebeault.com

Follow on Social Media, she'd love to hear from you!

 facebook.com/mhlebeaultauthor

 x.com/mhlebeault

 instagram.com/mhlebeault

 amazon.com/author/mhlebeault

 bookbub.com/authors/marie-helene-lebeault

 goodreads.com/mhlebeault

 linkedin.com/in/mhlebeault

 tiktok.com/@mhlebeaultauthor

ALSO BY THE AUTHOR

North Pole University - NA Paranormal Romance

Holiday Shifters

Freshman Frost

Sophomore Solstice

Junior Jinx

Senior Spark

Wedded Bliss

Mistletoe Misfits

Legends Reborn - NA Fairytale Retellings

A Curse of Snow and Ash

A Curse of Thorns and Slumber

A Curse of Glass and Shadows

A Curse of Scars and Silver

The Chronicles of the Starborne Cadets - YA Space Opera

Confluence of Destinies (Prequel)

Stars Beyond Realms

Shadows of Orion

Echoes of the Void

The Nebula's Heart

The Starborne Paradox

Defenders of the Realm - YA Epic Fantasy

A Journey to Power

The Quest for the Emerald Rattleback

A Summer of Discovery

The Quest for the Sacred Tree

A Summer of Opposites

The Quest for the Phantom Feather

A Summer of Courage

The Quest for the Kraken's Ink

A Summer of Destiny

The Quest for the Cursed Mirrors

A Summer of Unity

Defenders of the Realm - Special Edition Hardcover Set

The Evers Series - YA Science Fantasy

The Ancestors' Key

The Academy

The Time Walker

The World Jumper

5th Anniversary Edition Omnibus

The Traveler's Handbook

The Lost Key

Blood Magick Trilogy - YA Urban Fantasy

The Blood Mage

Blood Magick

Blood Legacy

Extended Edition Omnibus

Standalones

Clarity Castle

What Happens Next?

Ghost Stories

Echoes of Tomorrow

Utopia

Picture Books

Fairy Grandmother: Millie Goes to Antarctica

Fairy Grandmother: Millie Goes to the North Pole

Fairy Grandmother: Millie Goes to China

Fairy Grandmother: Millie Goes to Africa

(Also available in French, Spanish, German, and Italian)